The
BLACKOUT
gang

The BLACKOUT gang

JOSH McCALL

razor
bill

The Blackout Gang

RAZORBILL

Published by the Penguin Group
Penguin Young Readers Group
345 Hudson Street, New York, New York 10014, U.S.A.
Penguin Group (USA) Inc., 375 Hudson Street, New York, New York 10014, U.S.A.
Penguin Group (Canada), 90 Eglinton Avenue, Suite 700, Toronto,
Ontario, Canada M4P 2Y3 (a division of Pearson Penguin Canada Inc.)
Penguin Books Ltd, 80 Strand, London WC2R 0RL, England
Penguin Ireland, 25 St Stephen's Green, Dublin 2, Ireland
(a division of Penguin Books Ltd)
Penguin Group (Australia), 250 Camberwell Road, Camberwell,
Victoria 3124, Australia (a division of Pearson Australia Group Pty Ltd)
Penguin Books India Pvt Ltd, 11 Community Centre, Panchsheel Park,
New Delhi - 110 017, India
Penguin Group (NZ), Cnr Airborne and Rosedale Roads, Albany,
Auckland 1310, New Zealand (a division of Pearson New Zealand Ltd)
Penguin Books (South Africa) (Pty) Ltd, 24 Sturdee Avenue, Rosebank,
Johannesburg 2196, South Africa

Penguin Books Ltd, Registered Offices: 80 Strand, London WC2R 0RL, England

10 9 8 7 6 5 4 3 2 1

Library of Congress Cataloging-in-Publication Data is available

Printed in the United States of America

PROLOGUE

In a mansion on Manhattan's Upper East Side, a massive marble sculpture swayed back and forth. It crashed to the floor in a thunderous cloud of debris. On the way down, the sculpture struck a piece of Danish furniture. Glass shattered. Wood splintered. The floor shook as if an earthquake had hit.

No one was present but the mastermind and his friend. With a sly grin, they agreed it was a perfect beginning. Their dastardly scheme had been set into motion. And yet there was still so much to *do*.

They set to work.

One hundred miles away, on Pine Rock Mountain, three twelve-year-olds were stuck at summer camp. They had no idea they would soon meet face-to-face with the mastermind and become known as the Blackout Gang—famous beyond their wildest dreams.

At the moment, their only challenge was the humidity.

PINE ROCK MOUNTAIN

"Okay, here's the deal," Balthazar Bell announced, tucking a skinny arm behind his head. "My problem with Hollywood movies is that the smart people in them are always evil. Or at least messed up emotionally."

Balthazar—known to his friends as "BB"—waited, but Monica said nothing. He didn't really expect her to; she was too intent on her instrument.

BB chuckled. He could have told Monica that intelligent people were normally cast as pterodactyls in Hollywood movies. She wouldn't have blinked.

He heard her pluck a string on her Stradivarius and crank a tuning peg. He shifted around some more, trying to get comfortable on the cot: *impossible*! The cot, probably olive-colored once, was now yellow and fraying—and it smelled awful. It was at least as old as the shack that the camp called its library.

Ha! BB thought. *A library?* It was just a house of sticks. Something built by the Three Little Pigs.

BB yawned. He was pretty sure he'd never been this bored before. Ever. He pulled out his camera phone, the EXP3. Idly leaning on a button, he snapped several dozen identical pictures, then deleted them all without even bothering to look. There was a rule against cell phones at the camp, but BB still had his EXP3. He'd hidden it from the counselors, though he was no longer sure why he bothered. There was only enough signal up here for him to retrieve messages. So despite all its unusual and sweet features—many of which he'd rigged himself from parts scavenged from a Dumpster behind a Radio Shack—BB's phone couldn't perform its most basic function. It couldn't make calls.

No loss, he thought. The only two people he would ever want to phone were at camp with him anyway.

BB sighed. Here they were, a couple of twelve-year-olds hiding out in the library so that Monica could practice her violin—or rather tune it—and he could avoid socializing. He took off his glasses and rubbed his eyes.

"This is a totally sad place to be, y'know?" he pointed out.

Monica nodded as best she could while holding her violin between her chin and shoulder. She plucked another string, twisted a peg. BB knew she was grumpy too. She liked four hours a day with her Stradivarius, minimum, and the camp didn't allow her enough time with her instrument. Instead they held mandatory arts-and-crafts events or campfire sing-alongs or, BB shuddered, *sharing sessions,* all three of which seemed like a colossal waste of time.

"With all this rain," Monica grumbled, "I couldn't tune a flügelhorn, much less a Stradivarius." She played half a scale and returned to tuning. "What were you saying, BB?"

"That movies always show geniuses as unhappy people, or crazy people, or just, like, uncool. Like *Good Will Hunting, A Beautiful Mind, Amadeus.*"

"Hate to break it to you, *bubbeleh,*" Monica said, "but Matt Damon is totally cool, plus he gets the girl in the end. How's that fit with your cockamamie theory?"

BB could have listed a dozen other movies to prove his

point. He had an incredible memory for names, numbers, just about anything. But he was bored and didn't feel like going through the trouble.

"Okay," he said to Monica, "bad example. But you get my point. This depiction of intelligent people is not just mean to the likes of you and me, but it makes the children who are less intelligent than the two of us—"

Monica coughed. "And Kev1n," she reminded him.

"Than you and me and Kev1n," BB corrected himself. "It makes those other kids figure that if they were smart, then they'd be socially backward or have crippled hearts. They don't see how cool it is to be us or get, like, how happy we are."

Monica straightened and tuned. In the gruesome green flicker of the library's fluorescent light, her round face was lit like an unripe pumpkin. Her frizzy hair resembled shrubbery.

"Are we happy?" she asked her friend.

BB fidgeted a little, banged his heel against the cot. "Yeah, of course." He removed his hat, an old New York Giants baseball cap, and scratched at his closely cropped hair—a summer crew cut that Monica said made him look like a baby duck. "Aren't we?"

Monica shook her head. Her brown eyes were very serious. "Not here," she said.

BB made a small sound of disgust. "Well, no. Of course not *here*."

Monica raised her bow to her instrument. She dashed off a few quick arpeggios. The violin hit a sour note and Monica winced. "Ugh!"

BB blinked a few times behind his glasses and wiped his palms on his jeans. He was thinking about yawning again when suddenly the library door was flung open.

"Aha!" Someone laughed. "I knew I'd find you here."

BB turned. A trim boy, dressed in baggy shorts and high-top sneakers, stood in the doorway.

"Kev1n!" he and Monica shouted.

BB remembered the day he and Monica met Kev1n Park. They were entering fifth grade at the Maximillian S. Scholes Academy for the Bright and Talented.

Most of the kids at Scholes were identical, like boys or girls made of gingerbread—preppy clothes, perfect hair, strict schedules. . . . But Monica and BB were different, a little more eccentric than the average student, a lot more "bright and talented."

Then Kev1n showed up in homeroom one morning,

very tall and very athletic: an apparent jock at a school built for arts and science nerds. BB quickly discovered Kev1n was not your typical jock. He was as smart as anyone else at Scholes. He also just happened to be muscular, nimble, and, though Monica and BB would never say it out loud, a lot more photogenic than your typical Scholes nerd. He had an amazing gift for solving physics problems—issues of time and space, size and speed—which, if BB thought about it, probably contributed to Kev1n's excellence on his beloved BMX bike.

Just two weeks into that school year, Monica, Kev1n, and BB became fast friends. Unlike their supposedly "bright and talented" peers, they spent very little time worrying about their clothes. All of them dressed sloppily. They shunned the labels their rich classmates flaunted, and Monica looked like she hadn't successfully gotten a comb through her tangled curly mop since the last millennium.

Her sole concession to jewelry was her silver necklace with its Star of David, which the prime minister of Israel had bestowed upon her last spring after her debut with the symphony in Tel Aviv.

Though their thoughts and interests seemed wildly

different, the three friends were, as BB's mom would say, like peas in a pod. They spent most of their free time brainstorming cooperative ventures (or "scheming," as BB's suspicious parents called it).

If what BB had said earlier was true, that the three of them were in fact happy . . . well, that was in large part because of Kev1n. He was, in a sense, the only one who wasn't an obvious child sensation. Monica was freakishly good at music. BB's computer skills had landed him a job IT consulting for his dad's energy firm. But Kev1n's standout talents were more intuitive, more physical. This made him spectacular at things that the rest of the world apparently valued, like sports, which led him to being popular in "the scene" at Scholes. Everyone, even bullies, wanted to be friends with Kev1n.

Luckily for BB and Monica, Kev1n wasn't very interested in hanging out with athletes. Only BB and Monica met him on his own intellectual turf, satisfying his manic curiosity about the world, his appetite for adventure.

Yes, more than enjoying each other, the three friends needed each other. Kev1n made both BB and Monica seem *slightly* less geeky. Slightly less odd. While they, in turn, encouraged him to be more of an original.

Kev1n advanced into the camp's library. He nodded hello at Monica, then pointed toward the desktop computer in the corner of the shack. "I thought you'd be online"—he smirked at BB—"getting us in more trouble."

BB shook his head. "I can't be bothered. That's a 486 with a 14.4 modem. From before the Dark Ages. We'd grow old just waiting for it to boot up."

"Kev1n, I'm glad you're here," Monica said, still running her fingers over the violin's strings. "BB's been talking all kinds of *mishegoss*. I need you to set him straight."

BB was constantly amazed at how well Monica knew her instrument. She had been playing for so many years, she could tell if it was in tune by touch alone, without even hearing a note.

"So?" Kev1n snorted. "BB's full of hot air. What else is new?"

"Lay off, biker boy!" BB snapped, slapping at a horsefly that had landed on his leg.

"Whoa," Kev1n said, "chill out, man. I didn't mean—"

BB already regretted his words. Kev1n never meant any offense by his teasing. It was just his way.

"I'm sorry, Kev." BB sighed. "It's just this place." He

threw his hands out in a gesture that took in the library, the cabins, the quad, the entire camp, and all of Pine Rock Mountain. "Nature brings out the worst in all of us."

"True. Remind me how long we've been here," Kev1n said.

BB groaned. "Feels like years."

"It's been two weeks," Monica said.

Kev1n shot her a look of disbelief.

"Two weeks? That's it?" BB asked, incredulous. "You mean we're only half done with our sentence?"

"Cruel and unusual." Kev1n shook his head. "I don't know what our parents were thinking when they sent us here."

"Me neither," Monica agreed. "But it was something like, we need more experiences with normal kids our age."

"They were thinking," BB said, addressing Kev1n, "that you and me and Mon were becoming a menace to society."

"What? Because of the Fort Knox thing?" Monica asked.

Five months ago, the three of them had decided it would be funny to "break into" Fort Knox by hacking its computer system.

BB had insisted that first they come up with hacker handles. He, of course, had been using "BB" for years. He suggested Kevin use Kev1n, on the theory that long, complicated handles were a sure sign of an amateur. Monica, however, had never been able to settle on a nickname. In the end she remained plain old "Mon."

They released their hoax virus on St. Patrick's Day. It did nothing but blink a short message on all the Fort Knox computer terminals, wishing "all those working at the end of the rainbow the best of luck protecting their pots of gold." BB thought it was hilarious. The government, apparently, did not.

They did let the kids off, though, after BB explained, in detail, exactly how they had broken into the network in the first place.

Kev1n agreed with BB. "This is our punishment. They're grounding us while we reconsider our actions."

"And that's totally unfair!" Monica argued. "I wasn't even involved, not really."

"Oh, please," Kev1n said.

"Yeah," BB chimed in. "You helped us decode those tone patterns in, like, zero hours. Remember? Without you, we wouldn't have gotten anywhere."

"You were awesome," Kev1n said.

"Thanks." Monica smiled and abruptly turned her gaze floorward. "But I kept telling you guys that it wasn't worth it. Fort Knox has zero sense of humor."

"You were right," BB acknowledged solemnly.

"Still," Kev1n asked, "do you regret any of it?"

"Well . . ." Monica trailed off, still thinking about it.

"Me neither," Kev1n said.

There was a loud *slap!* They all jumped. Monica's book of classical music, which had been curling in the humidity, had fallen from her music stand.

"Oh. My. God!" Monica stalked toward the stand. She picked up her book and discovered its cover had ripped. "I hate this placc!" she yelled, her face red. "I hate it!"

Kev1n spread his arms wide. "In that case, I think you'll be pleased to hear my plan."

"A plan?" BB asked.

"*You* have a plan?" Monica was wary. "This won't be good."

"I just found out," Kev1n explained, "that we can have overnight campouts. Off by ourselves."

They looked at him blankly. "So?"

"So we go and we sign up to camp out in the woods

tonight along the upper lawn. But we don't go there; instead we get *off* this mountain." Kev1n paused to let the idea sink in.

"Wait," BB said. "Won't someone figure out what we're up to?"

Kev1n shook his head. "Nope. We're not *that* far from Manhattan. We'll just come back in the morning like we've been camping, and nobody will know any different."

"So . . . we ride our bikes down to the train?" asked Monica. "We take the train to the city?"

"Exactly." Kev1n grinned.

"And what do we do once we're there?" BB asked. "We can't go home."

Kev1n shrugged. "Mon finds a good place to play her violin while we go check out Chelsea Piers or something. I don't know. I haven't worked it out that far yet."

"Chelsea Piers? You are not going bowling, skating, and rock climbing," Monica declared. "Not without me."

"Come on, guys!" BB said. "This all sounds great, but we can't really skip out on camp. Our parents would be furious. Who knows what they would do?"

•　　　•　　　•

Remembering this days later, after everything had already happened, BB would think how it all might have ended right there. That is, if the three of them had never gotten involved in the events that were about to unravel.

If only BB had followed the rules and left his EXP3 at home. But he hadn't, and just then the phone started shuddering.

"A message!" BB yelled, suddenly merry. "You guys! A message from civilization!"

2

NEWT LIZZARD

If Monica was anything, she was tough. Strapped into a stroller as an infant, she'd been regularly wheeled along the streets of New York City's Chinatown. There, in the steamy summers, she grew accustomed to napping while rotting fish reeked from sidewalk stalls, while creatures with many tentacles and several eyes were stir-fried and sold on sticks. In her world travels as a touring violinist, she had eaten everything and anything without a second glance. She enjoyed true crime stories and had never experienced the slightest fear of mice, bees, or spiders.

Yet when the EXP3 buzzed and Monica read the call-back number off its screen, she flinched.

"Ew," she squealed. "Why is *Newt Lizzard* calling you?"

Monica, Kev1n, and BB all knew Newt. He was their classmate at Scholes. He was rich, arrogant, and obese. Not just chubby or even fat but strangely, *ridiculously* overstuffed.

Many other things about him were off-putting as well. His voice came forth in a whispery lisp, with an inflection that was jarring to the ear. His mumbled words seemed to swim in and out of focus. And he was always trying to bribe classmates into doing things for him, including being his friend.

Kev1n eyed BB with suspicion. "Newt Lizzard? You two aren't close, are you?"

"No!" BB yelped defensively. "I go to his house after school for study sessions. My mom makes me. And you know that."

Kev1n looked him up and down and nodded slowly. "Okay." He grinned. "I was just joking with you."

The three of them, like everyone else in the New York metropolitan area, were familiar with Newt's story. His parents, the Lizzards, were obscenely wealthy socialites who lived to see themselves in the papers. They had wed before a great many cameras. A year later, they had twins, a boy, Newton, and a girl, Sally. A year after that, the parents very publicly announced their intention to separate. Their divorce filled the tabloids for years. Sally was eventually awarded to her reluctant mother. Fat, peculiar Newt continued to live with his father in a mansion on Madison Avenue.

"Hey, is it true Newt has a private screening room for pre-release films?" Kev1n asked.

"Yeah," BB said.

"And a skate park on his roof?" Kev1n continued.

"Yeah. Not that Newt can use it," BB said, retrieving the message from his camera phone. "Can you imagine Newt on a skateboard?"

Kev1n and Monica frowned. Even with their superior intelligence, neither one of them *could* imagine it. Not in a million years.

BB punched a few more buttons, listened, then looked stunned. "Weird, you guys. Check this out."

Kev1n and Monica leaned forward. BB extended the EXP3 and pressed play. The message hissed and crackled.

"Goodness!" Monica gasped.

"What?" Kev1n asked. "You're hearing something?"

"Aren't you?"

He strained to listen. "I hear a fuzzy, whistling sound and something that sounds like scuffling. But that's it."

Monica shook her head. "I heard more than that."

"It's those ears of yours," Kev1n said. "You have, like, dog ears."

"How sweet of you to say," Monica growled through clenched teeth. "The message was from Newt. He was whispering. He sounded scared, I thought."

"Let's hear it again," Kev1n said. "Crank it up this time."

BB played it back at full volume. A crunch of distortion blasted through the camera phone's small speaker.

"Balthazaaar," Newt breathed. Even whispering, he lisped distinctively and displayed his usual lack of pitch. "It's me. There are some men here. Strange men . . ."

Glass smashed. Then faintly through the speaker they heard someone yell, "Oh no!" And a series of things crashed in the background.

"Ow!" a voice shouted, a voice that was suddenly far away, a voice that was frightened but still lisping and still recognizably the voice of Newt Lizzard.

"Ow, ow, ow! BB! *Help!*"

Newt gasped, then the call disconnected.

Monica, BB, and Kev1n stood in the library and wondered what to do. They could hear laughter in the distance. Their campmates and counselors were engaged in a three-legged race on the upper lawn. Monica imagined them hopping back and forth across a meadow, gaily tromping all the wildflowers.

"Okay," BB started, "I'm not saying anything, but I do happen to know that there's a city-bound express train departing Pine Rock Mountain at two forty-five."

"You memorized the train schedules?" Monica inquired.

BB shrugged. "It's not like it took a lot of effort."

Kev1n raised a skeptical eyebrow. "A two forty-five, huh? And Newt Lizzard is in peril." He tapped his lips thoughtfully. "Do I care?"

"C'mon," BB urged. "Newt's not that bad."

"He talks like a dcaf robot," Monica declared. "Is he even a mammal? Is he even from this solar system?"

"Hey!" BB half yelled. "Play nice. Just because the guy's got a few weight issues . . ."

"It's not just that he's . . ." Kev1n stopped, started again. "He's not just fat. He's strange. The guy takes being eccentric to a whole new level. I mean, maybe when he was a baby, someone dropped him on his big fat head."

Monica pursed her lips and thought about it some more. *Do I not like Newt because he's fat?*

No. It was something else, not the size of him, but his gravity.

"Newt," Monica finally decided, "is a *shmendrik*. He's just so dense around people. . . . He's like, I don't know—what's something that's really dense?"

"A rock?" BB volunteered.

"No," Kev1n jumped in, his face shining. "A neutron star."

Monica rolled her eyes. Typical Kev1n. So dramatic. Physics talk tended to make him a little light-headed.

"Newt Lizzard is not dense. He's a programming genius—brighter than the three of us combined." BB turned to Kev1n. "This is just like what I was telling Monica before you came in. Hollywood makes smart people out to be evil geniuses or emotional nincompoops. You're doing the same thing, assuming that just because Newt's really smart and a little chubby that he must be a bad guy."

Kev1n shook his head. "Who's calling Newt an evil genius? I'm not even convinced he's all that smart."

"Take my word for it," BB said. "I've seen some of the algorithms he's working up. They make our Fort Knox stunt look about as hard as selling Girl Scout cookies."

Monica felt impatient. "Can we focus?" she asked sternly. "Are we catching the two forty-five for Grand Central or aren't we?"

She and BB looked to Kev1n. "What happened to 'our parents will be so furious'?" he asked.

"*You* want to keep hanging around on Pine Rock Mountain?" Monica challenged.

"No!" BB and Kev1n answered together.

"All right, then," she said, very deliberately folding up her music stand. "We go with Kev's plan, hop a train to the city, and check on BB's friend. Who knows, maybe he *is* in trouble."

"I keep telling you, he's not *really* my friend," BB protested.

"Yeah," Kev1n said, "let's just hope he's not *really* in trouble, either."

Outside the library tent, the campsite was hot and humid. Monica looked at BB and could see him squinting in the glare. Gray clouds gathered overhead.

The three friends followed the birch tree trail back to their cabins. They packed up their backpacks and then, with Kev1n in the lead, cut diagonally across the quad in the direction of the main office. Monica and BB waited outside. Kev1n went in to add their names to the sign-up sheet for that night's campout.

Squirrels scampered about in the harsh sunlight. Scavenger birds stared from the barbecue pits. Feeling suddenly nervous, Monica swung her backpack hand to hand. "I know you say Newt's not such a bad guy, and I hope he's not hurt or anything, but *why*?" she whined. "Why did he have to call *us*?"

BB shrugged and shooed away a bumblebee. "Newt has no friends. Who else is he going to call?"

Monica frowned. "Good point."

Kev1n rejoined them, gave them the thumbs-up.

"BB, can I use your phone?" Monica asked.

BB looked at his EXP3 and shook his head. "There's still not enough signal to make an outgoing call. Besides, who do you need to talk to?"

"My mom and dad," Monica answered. "So that they know what's going on. I don't want them hearing we've gone AWOL and start freaking out."

"First of all, we'll be back tomorrow morning. No one will know we were gone," Kev1n stated. "Second, what are you going to tell them? That we're sneaking out of camp to go chase robbers?"

They crossed to the pay phone beside the energy drink dispenser. "Kev1n," Monica explained, "my parents are reasonable. As long as I tell them I need a night in the city, they'll be fine with it."

It was true. Monica had grown up jetting from concert to concert—sometimes on her own—in different foreign lands. She could tell her parents she was taking flying lessons and they wouldn't mind, so long as they knew beforehand.

She placed two quarters in the phone and dialed her number. "I'm getting the answering machine," she told the two boys.

She hung up without leaving a message and tried her parents' cell phones. Both numbers rolled over to an automated greeting. She replaced the receiver in the cradle and turned around.

"You're not even going to leave a message?" BB asked.

A look of concern crossed Monica's face. "No. I was going to, but I—I got distracted."

"Distracted?" BB asked. "By what?"

"It's probably nothing. It's just—I heard a bounce back."

"A what?" Kev1n asked.

"A bounce back," BB explained. "Like an echo."

"What's bizarre," Monica continued, "is I heard it during Newt's message too."

BB gave her a significant look. "You heard it on the camp phone *and* the EXP3?"

Monica nodded.

"You think someone's bugging our phone calls?" BB asked.

"After Fort Knox, you're surprised?" Monica answered.

"I didn't hear any echo on Newt's message," said Kev1n.

Monica's cheeks grew red with embarrassment. "It was up around thirty-five thousand hertz."

"Our hearing only extends to about twenty thousand," BB reminded Kev1n. He looked around wildly at the trees and cabins. "What if we're being taped right now? They've probably got surveillance cameras on all of us."

Kev1n sighed. "Only one way to find out. Let's go."

They followed him to the bike shed, where they rolled open the wide wooden doors and found their bikes.

"I don't like being watched," said BB, eyes darting back and forth. "I'm a very private person."

They spun the combinations on their bicycle locks.

"If they *are* watching us, think of it as an honor," Kev1n advised. "I mean, how many twelve-year-olds have the distinction of being watched by anyone but their parents?" He popped open his lock and wrenched loose his bike. He mounted it, then stood on the pedals, balancing like an acrobat. Giving Monica and BB a smile, he shot through the shed's doorway, skidding to a stop in a cloud of dust. "Come on!" Kev1n laughed over his shoulder. "Newt is in danger!"

As a rallying cry, it wasn't much, but it would have to do. Monica and BB pulled their bikes free. They joined Kev1n, and together they descended the camp's gravel path to the highway.

To Kev1n, it often seemed that the sun shone more brightly whenever he was riding his silver bicycle, with its chrome surfaces and flashy accents. He pedaled hard and could feel the blood pulsing through his veins. He looked back at Monica, riding the brake on her red bike, and BB, cautiously guiding his own green one.

The three wended their way off Pine Rock Mountain. Kev1n entertained them on the way down by slamming up the sides of the embankment, leaping at the apex, and spinning around in midair. Or he would drop off the path and curl his silver bike up and down the lip of a drainage pipe. BB pulled out his EXP3, as he always did, to snap some shots of the fluid movements of Kev1n and his bike.

Performing tricks came naturally to Kev1n. He hardly had to concentrate. He knew that his friends admired this talent of his. But he admired their special skills as well: Monica's amazing musical ability and the way BB could write code that would stump the smartest professors.

Kev1n assumed that BB and Monica were just like him. Whenever they were doing the things they loved most, their minds relaxed, focused. Kev1n's martial arts instructor would probably call it Zen.

At the bottom of the mountain, they hit pavement. Kev1n felt like a caged animal set free, anxious to stretch his legs. He waved "so long" to his two friends and took off on his own, a blur of mercury moving in the direction of the train stop.

Trees and shrubs whizzed by as Kev1n worked the pedals. The wind on his face made him feel as if he was soaring—like a great silver bird.

He reached the bicycle racks at the station in no time flat. Too soon, as far as he was concerned. He hadn't even broken a sweat. Monica and BB pedaled up scveral minutes later.

"I just realized something," Kev1n told them as they dismounted. "We left our locks back at camp."

"So we did," Monica agreed, panting. "Pretty dumb for three brainiacs. Kev, can you ride back and get them?"

"No time," BB said. "The train's here in under six and a half minutes."

"Even I can't make it that fast," Kev1n agreed. "And I'm not leaving my bike here overnight unlocked."

"Me neither," Monica said.

"Fine," BB told them. "Let's just take them on the train."

"Can we do that?" Monica asked. "Isn't it against the rules?"

Kev1n smirked. "Since when do we care about the rules?"

They wheeled their bicycles up the platform, purchased "overnight excursion" tickets from a machine, and then stood with their backpacks, waiting in silence. BB took a few pictures to pass the time. He then stopped and glanced back toward the camp.

"What's wrong?" Kev1n asked.

"Nothing," BB said. "I just keep expecting to hear alarms sounding or see counselors driving down from the mountain to retrieve us."

"Not gonna happen," Kev1n said. "As far as anybody knows, we're off pitching a tent for the night."

"Sure," BB said, "but we're not pitching a tent. And for all we know, right now a counselor's strolling up the mountain to check on us, looking for our nonexistent campsite. And when we're found to be missing, what then? Everyone will fly into a manic panic. Our parents will be alerted. The police will be summoned. A huge deal will be made of everything."

Monica laughed. "BB, you are the most paranoid person I know."

"It could happen," BB insisted.

"What are you saying? That you want to turn back?" Kev1n asked.

BB opened his mouth, but before he had a chance to answer, the train arrived. It was as sleek and shiny as Kev1n's silver bicycle. Its doors opened, exhaling the heavenly frost of air-conditioning.

Unable to resist the lure of frigid goodness, the three of them stepped on board. They took their bikes to a luggage area, hung them off ceiling hooks, and grabbed seats nearby. They tossed their backpacks on the overhead racks and settled into their seats.

The doors hissed shut.

"Next stop," intoned a lady's electronic voice over the train's sound system, "New York City."

3

THE TWO FORTY-FIVE

The train sped down its track and Pine Rock Mountain melted away. A corridor of elm trees arched low over the train tracks, causing the view of the nearby town to flash at BB through the gaps.

Stone cottage. Firehouse. General store.

Then nothing.

Well, BB thought, *no turning back now. Might as well relax.*

All second thoughts vanished from his head as the train chugged harder, gaining speed. He touched the cold glass of the train window as more images blurred past.

A quarry. An overpass. A fenced-in lot full of broken neon signs.

Little by little, they were returning to a familiar landscape.

Asphalt and skyscrapers. Manhattan. Home.

"We should have a strategy," Kev1n said, interrupting BB's reverie. "I mean, after we get to Lizzard Mansion, then what?"

"A *strategy*? Why bother?" Monica asked sarcastically. "Let's just go stumbling into things. It'll be more dangerous that way."

"Seriously," BB said. He squirmed against the straight-back bench, picking nervously at its reddish upholstery. "It might be dangerous. We should at least allow for the possibility that whoever broke into the Lizzards' might still be there when we arrive."

Beneath the hood of his gray sweatshirt, Kev1n's eyes flashed. "We should also allow for the fact that they might have weapons. Trip wires, grenades, drone bombs, memory powders . . . We just don't know."

Monica rolled her eyes.

"What? They might be black belts in arnis or jujitsu," Kev1n continued. "Or they could have huge attack dogs with them. *Really* huge attack dogs, like, the size of SUVs!"

Monica snorted. "There's no breed of dog as big as an SUV."

"No?" Kev1n asked, looking at her quite seriously. "What if they're *genetically mutated* dogs?"

BB fidgeted uneasily with his Giants cap. "Stop joking," he said. "It might be dangerous, but genetically mutated dogs? Even *I'm* not that paranoid."

"Honestly, I think the joke is on us," Kev1n said. "I love an adventure as much as the next guy, but it still seems to me that Newt's making all this up."

"Why would he do that?" Monica asked.

"Oh, I don't know," Kev1n said. "Maybe because he's lonely. Like we'd be if we didn't have each other. He lives on the top floor of that mansion, pretty much by himself. He doesn't even have any friends except for BB. And BB won't admit to *being* his friend."

"He has his nanny," BB said. "They're really close. But she's, like, ancient. And Turkish."

"Where's his dad?" Monica asked.

"Always off somewhere," BB answered.

"He races cars," Kev1n remembered.

"Among other things, yeah," BB confirmed. He turned to look out the train window. A series of homes drifted by, with trailers in the front yards and clotheslines in the back.

"So he's been, like, abandoned by his parents?" Monica asked.

"Basically," BB said. "I mean, you know how grown-ups are."

They all had good relationships with their own parents, but that didn't mean they were blind to the immature things that *supposedly* adult people did.

"Not to change the subject," Kev1n said, "but do you think we'll have time to check out Newt's rooftop skate park? I heard it overlooks the polar bear pond at the Central Park Zoo!"

"Come on," Monica said. "This might not be all fun and games. Newt did sound scared on the message."

"Exactly." BB paused, withdrew the EXP3 from his backpack, and snapped a few pictures of the town they were rolling through.

"Tickets! Tickets!" a deep voice called. The conductor appeared, clicking his hole puncher. He was a barrel-chested man with a kind face. He wore an immaculate blue uniform and smelled of roasted almonds, the kind you could only buy at Grand Central.

"Tickets?" he asked. Kev1n, BB, and Monica handed him theirs. The conductor squinted at the three adolescent passengers as he punched their slips. "A bit young to be making this trip alone, aren't you?"

"We have no choice," BB said. "We're on a mission— rescuing a classmate from almost certain danger."

"A mission?" The conductor absorbed this. His mouth twitched at the corners as he fought hard not to laugh.

Monica folded her hands in her lap and looked sweetly at the big man. "Mom's in the bathroom," she said. "A couple of cars down."

"Very good, then," the conductor said, beaming.

He clicked his hole puncher in approval, then fixed BB with an overly grave look. "Good luck with your mission there, little soldier."

"Thanks." BB frowned.

The big man chuckled as he moved on to the next car, taking the odor of almonds with him.

"Nice job on the cover-up, dweeb," Kev1n growled.

"I hate lying," BB said flatly. "Besides, it's not like adults ever believe you when you're telling the truth."

"You hate lying? *You?*" Kev1n asked. "*Wired* magazine's Hacker of the Year for three years running?"

"It's not the same," BB argued.

Monica cleared her throat. "Boys, please. We're supposed to be making a *strategy*, not snipping at each other. Why don't we figure out who could have done something to Newt? Let's start by making a list of everyone who doesn't like him."

"Okay," said Kev1n. He leaned forward, elbows on his knees. "There's you. There's me. There's the rest of the school. Who else? Oh, his parents, it sounds like."

BB looked out the window as the train continued its journey south, gently meandering up a slope, then climbing down into a wide valley. Off to their right, the Hudson River gleamed silver as a sword in the afternoon sun. He snapped pictures of the blue herons and snowy white egrets along the riverbank with his EXP3 phone. He turned and took a few of the speedboats moored near the opposite shore.

A cruise ship glided up the river, the overnight run from New York to Albany. He took a few snaps of that as well. Then he glanced down.

"Hey!" he said. "We finally have a signal!"

"Call Lizzard Mansion," Monica said. "Maybe the police are there. Then we won't have to bother."

BB dialed Newt's number. He let it ring and ring. Eventually he hung up.

"No one's answering," BB said.

"Maybe Newt's being held hostage," Monica suggested. "I mean, his dad is like one of the richest people on the planet, right? Imagine the ransom."

"The security for Lizzard Mansion is just unbelievable," BB said. "Retinal scans, key codes, all that. How could anyone, kidnapper or otherwise, get in?"

"Maybe it was an inside job?" Monica suggested. "You know, someone who works for Mr. Lizzard."

Kev1n held up an index finger. "Suspect number one, the nanny from Turkey. What's her name again?"

"Ankara Braceling," BB said. "Though Newt calls her Ankle Bracelet because she keeps him under house arrest. She never lets him out of her sight."

BB didn't say it, but Ankara was probably the closest thing to *real* family that Newt had.

"Shhh!" Monica silenced the boys with a gesture. Her eyes were shut in concentration.

"What is it?" Kev1n asked.

"Someone's talking about us," she replied.

"You mean we're being watched?" BB whispered.

Kev1n leapt up to grab the bars of the overhead luggage racks. Dangling there, he cast his gaze up and down the car. He pointed out two passengers sitting a few rows back in the same car, an older woman and a young blond girl. Each was dressed formally, in a long dress, with white cotton gloves, and each wore her hair pinned up in an old-fashioned style.

"Them?" Kev1n asked skeptically.

BB leaned into the aisle. "They look harmless to me," he said. "Just some old lady hauling her poor granddaughter into the city for an evening of theater or something."

"Harmless, sure . . ." Monica said. "Until they come over and start asking us a bunch of questions about what we're up to. Next thing you know we're on the next train back to Pine Rock Mountain."

"No way." Kev1n smirked. "They don't even know who we are."

The woman caught Monica's glance, stood, and approached.

"Miss Steen!" the woman exclaimed, wobbling up the aisle with the blond girl in tow. "Miss *Monica* Steen?"

Kev1n gulped.

"Guess again," Monica said. "They do know who we are!"

"Great," BB yelped. "So who are *they*? FBI? CIA? Department of Homeland Security?"

"Calm down," Monica whispered. "I'll handle this."

The woman arrived at their seats. "Miss Steen, I presume." The woman's attitude was smug. She was evidently more familiar with making demands than with asking questions.

"That's me." Monica climbed to her feet to head off the woman's advance.

"We saw you at Lincoln Center the night the New York City Ballet performed their pas de deux to your sonata."

"Oh. I didn't realize I had *fans* on board." Monica glanced over at her friends.

BB exhaled in relief.

"That performance was fun," Monica continued.

"Fun? It was magical, dearie, simply magical." The woman's heavily made-up eyelids fluttered for a second, as if in contented recollection, then flew open again. "I must admit," she said, with more than a trace of disapproval in her voice, "that we recognized you now only because you appear to be wearing the *exact same outfit* you wore that evening."

"Right, well." Monica looked down at her ordinary clothes: slacks, blouse, sneakers. "This is what I wear," she said, without apology. "It's comfortable."

The train swerved sharply, catching the woman and girl by surprise. They teetered on their heels and threw their arms out to maintain balance.

Outside the window, the sooty brick and stripped billboards of the Bronx passed. The train left behind the Hudson and cut east toward the Triborough Bridge.

"Hey!" BB whispered during the confusion. "Ditch your adoring public, Mon. They could start asking questions."

"Well," Monica said in farewell, "almost there. We'd all better take our seats. It was nice meeting you."

"Nonsense," the woman barked. "Considerable time remains." She straightened her hat and tugged on her gloves. "Now, then, where is your Stradivarius? I daresay, you are not traveling without it?"

Monica sank into her seat and pointed overhead at her backpack, bulging with her instrument case. "There." She sighed.

The woman nodded with satisfaction.

The train rattled, louder and louder now, traveling onto the bridge, nearing Manhattan.

The woman raised her voice. "Miss Steen. I need you to take on a pupil. My niece here." She flicked her hand at the blond girl, who stood mortified and silent beside the woman.

Monica screwed up her face in disbelief. "A pupil?"

"I am quite prepared to pay you the going rate, and I daresay I won't take no for an——"

Just then, quite abruptly, the two forty-five to Grand Central screeched to a halt.

"Now what?" the woman asked, of no one in particular.

"It stopped," Kev1n answered.

"Of course it stopped, young man," the woman chided him.

"No, not just the train," said BB worriedly. "*Everything* stopped."

It was true. Not only was the train dead, but so were its lights and air-conditioning. Almost immediately, the darkened car began to heat up under the August sun.

"Terrorists!" the woman squealed, imagining the worst. "Oh, don't panic, children! Don't panic!"

Kev1n, who was nearest to the window, grasped the metallic clasp at the base of the frame and pulled it across hard to the right. The window slid open. Outside, the temperature was still in the nineties and the humidity remained stifling. Below the bridge, the Harlem River glistened.

The blond girl bit her lip and glanced around nervously. "How are we going to get out?"

"Train doors are unsealed whenever the power cuts out," BB told her.

"So we're not stuck?" Monica asked.

Kev1n sized up the situation. "Nah," was all he said.

The old woman and the blonde sank into seats across the aisle. In a voice full of fear, the woman kept warning everyone not to be afraid.

Gesturing at her with a thumb, Kev1n addressed the blond niece. "Can you calm her down? Shoot her with a tranquilizer dart or something?"

In the dim half-light, they saw the blonde smile.

BB tried to use his EXP3 to dial into a headline news service, but his call was unsuccessful. All circuits were busy. Luckily, the official explanation wasn't long in coming.

"Ladies and gentlemen," the conductor shouted, stepping into their car. "We apologize for this unscheduled stop, but the rails are currently without power. Rescue workers have been notified of our situation and will arrive shortly with buses to take everyone the rest of the way into Midtown. So please, be patient. Be calm, and everyone will be out of here and on their way as quickly as possible."

All of this succeeded remarkably well in convincing the three twelve-year-olds not to try anything rash. Until the conductor closed his speech with the following suggestion: "Get to know your neighbor. It'll help pass the time." He strode past, continuing on to the next car.

BB gulped. Get to know your neighbor? They were New Yorkers! Talking to the people around you was just—*unnatural*. Besides, their nearest "neighbors" were the annoying woman and her niece, who already knew way too much.

Monica, BB, and Kev1n looked over at the matronly old lady, who was now weeping into a silk handkerchief. They shuddered in horror.

"We're outta here," Kev1n declared. He snatched up his backpack and crossed to the luggage area. Without speaking, the other two did the same. They pulled down their bicycles.

The three of them rolled their bikes to the front of the car. Once there, as BB had predicted, they had little difficulty in prying open the train door. Kev1n went first, and the other two followed, lifting their bikes and hopping down onto the rocky bed of the train bridge.

BB looked around. The complex structure of the bridge was enormous. Where they stood, several railroad tracks ran side by side.

Should the power return, he realized, another train could come barreling down any of these tracks from either direction. Walking where pedestrians were not allowed was, he felt, at one and the same time, very brave and very, very stupid.

Rather than mount their bikes and risk popping a tire or losing control on the uneven, rocky surface, they made their way to the end of the bridge on foot. When they rolled their bikes onto 125th Street, each of them was smiling.

Manhattan. They were finally home.

But their smiles didn't last.

"Uh, Kev1n," BB began.

"Yeah?" Kev1n answered.

"Are you noticing what I'm noticing?"

Kev1n glanced around. "What?"

Traffic in the neighborhood was snarled and slowed to a crawl. Horns blared. Drivers yelled at each other in the sticky heat.

"The traffic lights. They're all out," BB said.

"First the train? Now the electricity for the traffic lights? What's going on?" Monica wailed.

"Must be a blackout," Kev1n said. He smiled. "New York City without power? This is going to be serious fun."

4

THE ELVII

The three friends sought out a quieter side street.

"A blackout," Monica repeated. "What do we do now?"

"Exactly what we planned before the blackout started," Kev1n said. "Lct's gct over to Newt's house!"

He took off on his bicycle, then turned and pedaled back. "Where is Newt's house anyway?"

"Sixty-eighth Street and Madison," BB answered.

Monica considered this. They were at 125th Street. In Manhattan, twenty north-south blocks equaled a mile. That meant they still had almost three miles to go.

As her *bubbe* would say, "Oy."

"We should keep in mind that people will be absolutely everywhere," BB said. "Offices will be shut down. Everyone will be trying to walk home. Millions and millions of people."

Monica sighed. "And without the traffic lights, it'll be total chaos. There might even be looting!"

"Sounds rad," Kev1n said, pulling his bike up on its back wheel and hopping it up and down. "We can get around the crowds. Just follow me."

"Okay, but go slow," Monica warned.

"I will. Don't worry."

They mounted their bicycles, pedaling south on Third Avenue. Kev1n began leading them in a crisscross pattern through the city. He seemed to know exactly where the crowds *wouldn't* be. But it quickly became obvious that what Kev1n considered a leisurely pace was grueling for the other two.

"Slow down!" gasped BB.

Ahead of them, lost in his own world, Kev1n accelerated around taxis, jumped curbs, and skidded his back tire on the sidewalks.

Desperately pursuing him, they turned right on 119th to continue down Lexington Avenue. Kev1n was already a block ahead.

Monica, stupid with frustration, tried to copy Kev1n's careless cool. She clumsily hopped a curb but succeeded only in bumping her bike chain off its sprocket. She dismounted her vehicle, glared hotly at the limp chain, and proceeded to push. Always nice, BB followed suit.

This was the kind of situation in which the two of them *especially* needed Kev1n. They might be brilliant with computer code or violin concertos, but the simplest tasks—changing a lightbulb, for example, or fixing a loose bike chain—were utterly beyond them. Kev1n often joked that without his mechanical aptitude, Monica and BB would struggle just to open a door. Right now, it didn't seem so far from the truth.

"Remind me to tell Kev1n the meaning of slow," BB muttered.

"Right," Monica said, shoving tendrils of hair, slick with sweat, from her eyes.

She glanced around and noticed that they were passing through a particularly unsafe-looking neighborhood. Block after block of fenced-in lots, rubble, and half-finished apartment buildings. Everything felt suddenly, eerily deserted—void of pedestrians and cars. Many of the street-light bulbs were smashed on the sidewalks, and the parking meters had lost their heads. It made Monica decidedly uneasy.

"Think Kev1n will realize he lost us and double back?" she asked.

"Sure," BB answered, "about the time he gets to Lizzard Mansion. I'm hoping he'll at least wait for us before he goes in to save Newt."

They both laughed and nervously continued walking down the lonesome patch of upper Lexington Avenue. Overhead, a few clouds drifted across the sky, blotting out the sun. Their world fell into shadow.

They stopped as they noticed a group of boys, wearing long, dark coats and construction boots, emerging from one of the vacant buildings.

The boys formed a line across the street, blocking the path.

"Come on, BB," Monica said. "Let's go another way." She whirled around and found another line of boys behind her, blocking that route as well. She craned her neck, looking for Kev1n, but he was now out of sight. Hoping to avoid a nasty confrontation, she lowered her kickstand and dropped her hands to her side.

"Vay is mir," she said.

"Totally," BB agreed.

"Is there something we can help you with?" Monica called politely to the group of boys.

They ignored her inquiry. There were seven, maybe nine of them. Their faces were hard and their eyes cold.

"I don't like this at all," BB whispered to Monica. "Maybe we should make a break for—"

"Watta we got here?" one of the boys asked another.

The other replied with a hard, menacing stare toward BB. "Looks to me like we got an Elvis, Elvis."

"Oh no!" BB whispered frantically. "Monica, this is not good. Really, really not good."

"Why?" Monica asked.

"I've heard of these guys." BB trembled. "The Elvii—a gang of teenage runaways. I read about them online and in the *Post*. I thought they were just an urban legend."

"Oookay," Monica said slowly. "What's their story, these Elvii?"

"They roam the streets of New York, stealing, looting, whatever," BB panted. "All of them have police records a mile long. But they're all known by the same code name: Elvis."

"They sure don't dress like Elvis," Monica said. "In fact, they just look like thugs."

"Originally Elvis was the name they gave their victims because it was the worst insult they could think of," BB explained. "Eventually they started referring to each other that way too. One rumor had it that they all lived under the mayor's house, Gracie Mansion, in a secret lair called Gracieland. And they called their leader 'the King.'"

"King or not, they're coming this way," Monica whispered. "Don't freak out, and don't do anything dumb."

Two of the Elvii approached. Wordlessly each chose a bike and took hold of its handlebars. They raised the kickstands and wheeled the bikes away.

"Hey!" Monica protested. "Those are ours."

"Shhh," BB told her. "Better they take the bikes than . . ." He drew a finger across his neck.

The Elvis who had taken the red bike noticed its loose chain. "Eh. This one's busted." He kicked it. Monica's bicycle dropped to the ground with a crash.

"This one works pretty good," the other Elvis said. He mounted BB's green bike and began riding in circles. His coat flared out behind him like a cape.

Others in the gang approached Monica and BB and stood menacingly over them while two Elvii snatched their backpacks. The boys began pawing through the packs, mumbling about money, tossing the contents all over the street.

For a moment, none of them appeared to be paying the slightest attention to their two cowering captives.

"Maybe we should try to get away?" BB asked softly.

Just then, Monica saw them pull her violin case from her backpack. "Not a chance," she answered.

Monica took a step toward the Elvis holding her violin, but BB grabbed her by the arm and pulled her back.

"Hey," the Elvis called out, having opened the case. "A fiddle."

"It's a violin," BB corrected.

"It's whatever we say, Elvis." The Elvis took two steps and sharply socked BB in the stomach. "You don't talk that way to the King."

Monica gasped. BB was right. This guy was their leader—the King!

"Don't hit him!" she cried. "It's a fiddle *and* a violin— they're the same thing!"

"Oh, you don't want me to hit him? Okay." The King lifted his foot and kicked BB in the rear. "This is more fun anyway."

Monica flinched. BB stumbled forward and his glasses tumbled off his nose. The Elvis stooped and snatched them up. He examined the frames curiously for a moment before flinging them to the sidewalk and hopping in place. The lenses crunched underfoot.

"You're right." The King laughed. "This is much, much better than hitting him."

Everything turned blurry for BB. Without his glasses, he was practically blind. He crawled back toward Monica and could hear her whimpering.

"Don't worry," he whispered. "I always carry plenty of replacement pairs."

"It's not that," she replied. "They found your EXP3."

"What? Be careful with that!" BB shouted, unsure exactly where to look. "It's *very* fragile."

"Hey, I got an idea," the King said. "Let's play daredevil." He pointed at the violin and the EXP3. "Set up a ramp. Let's see if I can jump 'em."

Another Elvis snorted. "You're no good at daredevil."

"Yeah," piped up a third. "No way you'll clear them, King."

"I don't plan to clear them," the King announced from the seat of BB's bike. "I plan to *smash* them."

The others laughed.

Monica knelt and began collecting the contents of their backpacks. "Here," she said to BB, holding out a backup pair of spectacles.

BB put them on. His vision cleared and he focused on the scene before them. He stared in mute horror as the Elvii placed an orange-and-white construction barrel and a board in the street, creating a makeshift bike ramp. They put the EXP3 and Stradivarius down a short distance away, then formed a circle to cheer the destruction.

The King rode BB's bicycle a little way down the street. Then he turned and pedaled toward the ramp. Faster, faster. Faster!

Thump! The bike tires hit the ramp. The bike soared into the air. The King screamed happily. Still soaring, he came off the bicycle seat and yanked hard on the handlebars. The front tire rose. The King balanced the bike perfectly, intending it to land on the rear tire and, in the process, pulverize Monica's priceless violin! He guided the bike down, but instead of the expected crunch of splintered wood, the back wheel struck only pavement.

"What the—" the King yelped. He turned and found that someone had snatched away the Stradivarius and EXP3.

"Kev1n!" BB and Monica exclaimed.

Their friend had silently circled back, undetected by the Elvii. Having shed his sweatshirt, Kev1n now stood defiantly in the middle of the street, surrounded on all sides by the gang of runaways.

"Catch!" Kev1n tossed the EXP3 and Stradivarius to BB and Monica, then faced the Elvii, ready for whatever would come. To the Elvii, it must have looked like Kev1n had a death wish—but BB knew better.

The King hopped off the bike and let it fall. "Say your prayers, Elvis," he snarled, his expression suddenly savage. With a cry, he flew at Kev1n. The others joined in, doing what came naturally. They balled up their fists and attacked.

Kev1n raised his arms, flailing his elbows to block their blows. None got through. Kev1n hopped backward— once, twice, three times. Now his attackers were forced to shift and approach from the front. They came forward and Kev1n proceeded to counterattack.

He leaned far forward, as if bowing, kicked out a back leg, and swiveled nimbly around. The movement was graceful, totally unexpected, and brought Kev1n's foot straight into the face of his biggest attacker. There was a loud crunch. The Elvis howled from the impact and staggered away.

The others hesitated for a moment as the biggest Elvis retreated. They glared at each other, then rushed in. *All* of them. One Elvis managed to grab Kev1n around the shoulders, holding down his arms, hugging him tightly from behind.

"I got him!" the Elvis shouted. "I got—*oof!*"

Exploding with a strange, guttural yelp, Kev1n threw out both arms. He slid downward and twisted from the locking grip.

Outsized and outnumbered, working from a crouch so low that he was nearly kneeling, Kev1n seized his advantage. The Elvii were powerful fighters, but they all fought like boxers, planting their feet and throwing punches.

Kev1n fought like the tae kwon do expert that, in fact, BB knew he was. He frustrated them. They swung, often and hard, but their fists met only air. The boy was too fleet, too fluid, and too ready for their every move.

The Elvii, in contrast, appeared to be moving in slow motion.

Kev1n dealt with one Elvis at a time, dispatching each in turn with ruthless efficiency. After just one minute of scuffling, only two Elvii remained uninjured. The rest had risen from the avenue scraped and bruised, leaning on each other for support.

The two remaining Elvii charged at Kev1n. Both dove, grappling desperately for his waist. Kev1n leapt. He eluded their tackle, then delivered a roundhouse kick that went high, clobbering one Elvis hard in the chest. The air left the attacker's lungs with a *whoosh*. He clutched his chest, then walked away gasping for breath.

Kev1n now faced the last Elvis. The Elvis made a couple of feints in his direction, but Kev1n stood motionless. His face was calm and composed.

The Elvis threw a couple of additional jabs, then ran away to join his bruised and beaten companions.

The three twelve-year-olds stood alone in the middle of a deserted Lexington Avenue.

Monica had her Stradivarius and BB his EXP3.

Kev1n tiptoed around, stuck his head into doorways, ducked behind pillars, peered around corners. Then he turned to his friends.

"They're gone," he said, brushing his palms together. "The Elvii have left the buildings."

The three friends continued their journey to Lizzard Mansion's 68th Street location. After Kev1n had fixed her bike, Monica had taken charge. She'd dictated a course down the most-populated avenues. Kev1n, while bristling at the easy pace, didn't complain.

An hour later, they arrived at the mansion, a spectacular five-story home built on the world's most prime real estate. They pushed their bikes up the many marble steps of the outside stoop, approached the mansion's front door, and rang the doorbell.

Chimes played inside the mansion. They waited. No one answered.

They were about to give up when Kev1n reached for the doorknob, turned it, and found the door open!

"What? No alarm?" Monica asked.

BB frowned. "Maybe it's been disabled."

The three friends entered Lizzard Mansion slowly,

cautiously. The household was humming along . . . still powered.

"Probably a backup generator," BB explained.

They parked their bicycles inside the foyer, then BB led the way across the length of the hallway.

"Hey." Kev1n poked him in the ribs. "Check it out." He pointed to five cameras, mounted close to the ceiling.

BB nodded. "You're always under surveillance in Lizzard Mansion."

They approached an elevator. BB reached up and pressed the button. "And call me crazy, but I *still* say we were being watched up at camp too. Mon," he prodded, "you heard the bounce back on the phones. The EXP3 *and* the pay phone."

Monica acknowledged this warily. "Yeah."

"So somebody was listening in, to *both* phone calls."

"So?" She shrugged. "It could have been a coincidence or just a bad connection."

The elevator cage began its clattering descent.

"Does that really seem likely to you?" BB asked.

Monica remained silent, her mouth drawn in a grim line.

"I'm not saying that whoever was listening was out to

hurt us," BB argued. "But maybe someone is trying to keep tabs on us. Someone who knows that we know Newt."

Monica and Kev1n exchanged looks of concern. The elevator arrived, and its doors opened. They climbed aboard.

"Penthouse," BB said to the air. The elevator doors clattered shut. The cage rose.

"Dude." Kev1n's eyes roamed the elevator's shining, high-tech, fiber-optic walls. "This is sweet."

"Guys," Monica jumped in. "Before we geek out about the elevator, I need to make a few points about BB's theory. First, we don't know that anybody's *really* messing with Newt. Second, we don't know Newt *that* well. And third, BB, you're really starting to freak me out. So knock it off."

The elevator stopped at the top floor. Monica, BB, and Kev1n stood facing the closed elevator doors. Kev1n inched forward and positioned himself in a defensive posture.

"What are you doing?" Monica asked.

"Making myself ready for whatever's on the other side," Kev1n said. Then he blinked and relaxed his posture.

"It's a joke," he said. "Come on, Mon. I was trying to make you laugh."

"Ha. Ha," Monica deadpanned.

"No, really," Kev1n insisted. "There's nothing on the other side of this door but a slightly overweight kid who's looking for a little attention."

"Let's hope," BB said.

With a chime, the elevator doors slid open.

5

LIZZARD MANSION

Kev1n gasped.

Jokes aside—no amount of preparation would have readied him for the sight that mct his eyes.

There, in the great room outside the elevator, sat Newt Lizzard, a pale-skinned pudgeball in expensive clothes. But if he was looking for attention, he had certainly gone out of his way to get it.

The room around Newt bore clear signs of a struggle: chairs toppled, a sofa overturned. A weighty marble sculpture lying amid the remnants of a glass dining table . . .

Newt was handcuffed to his chair. He had a gag in his

mouth. And there was the smell of burning wood—logs crackling in a massive fireplace.

BB hurried over, sidestepping the splinters and shards, to untie Newt's gag.

"Newt, what happened?" he asked. "Are you okay?"

Newt sputtered and coughed.

"Well, it's about time," he droned in his nasally monotone, like a computer with a bad cold. He rattled the cuffs, which were wound around the arm of his chair. "I've been stuck here for six hours."

Newt's face, Kev1n noticed, was beginning to bruise. Someone had hit him, right below his left eye.

Was all of this *real*? he wondered. Had someone actually meant harm to Newt Lizzard?

Kev1n had to admit that in spite of his instinct about the situation, signs pointed to yes.

"You're welcome," Monica said tartly. "For saving you, I mean."

"Yes. Thanks," Newt said. "Now get me out of these." He jerked his chubby chin toward Kev1n, who'd remained in the corner nearest the elevator. "You! Go to my room." He nodded over his right shoulder, toward a doorway.

"Through there, first door on the left. In the top drawer of my desk, there's a set of lock picks."

Kev1n made no move to obey. Instead, struggling to make sense of the scene before him, he remarked sleepily, "We left our bikes downstairs. Hope that's okay."

Newt didn't register Kev1n's reply; he just fixed his gaze on BB. "You brought your EXP3, right? Start shooting images of *everything*, this room, that room there, and the downstairs hallway."

"Okay." BB paused. "Why?"

"Evidence!" Newt explained. "We'll gather clues that way."

BB's eyes went wide. "Right!" He unshouldered his backpack, extracted his camera, reversed the Giants cap on his head, and started to shoot pictures.

"Monica," Newt commanded as though he were a king and not a sweaty fat kid handcuffed to a dining room chair.

"What?" she replied coldly, clearly not enjoying the way she was being addressed.

"I'm famished."

Kev1n took a few steps toward Newt. He was beginning to sweat and wondered why anybody would have a fire lit on a sweltering August afternoon.

"We're pretty hungry ourselves," Kev1n said. "We've had quite an adventurous day, you know."

Newt ignored the comment. "Run to the kitchen, Monica, and make me a sandwich. Prosciutto and Emmenthal."

Beneath her damp, chaotic hair, Monica's eyes burned with outrage. "What?!" she asked.

BB briefly lowered the camera. "That means ham and cheese," he explained.

She waved aside her friend's translation and leaned in close to Newt's pasty face. "News flash, schmuck! We're not your servants."

"Speaking of which," Kev1n said, "where *are* the servants?"

Once again, Newt didn't respond.

Kev1n frowned. Why wouldn't Newt talk to him? *Everyone* wanted to talk to him.

"I asked you a question," Kev1n pointed out.

Newt rolled his eyes. "It's Thursday," he answered.

"So?" Kev1n challenged.

"Thursday's the staff's day off."

Kev1n paced the dining room. He could see that it aggravated Newt, so he went about it slowly. There was a lot of floor and a great many rugs. The room was as large as the cafeteria at their school.

"How convenient," Kev1n observed, "that this happened when you were alone."

"What about the Turkish woman?" Monica asked. "Your nanny?"

Newt blew out an exasperated breath. "Ankle Bracelet's on vacation." He glared around the room, at the dim corners and high ceilings. "Now, chop-chop, everyone. You have your tasks."

With defiant calm, Kev1n righted a chair, Monica righted another beside him, and they both sat, examining Newt. For a time, no one spoke. The only sounds in the room were the popping of the fire and the snapping of the digital shutter as BB dutifully photographed the areas Newt had indicated.

"First, tell us what happened," Monica demanded.

Just hours ago, Monica had wondered aloud whether Newt Lizzard was of this planet. Now, as Kev1n sat on the couch beside Monica, he began wondering the same thing.

Newt's head was oval, a perfect egg. His eyelids never blinked. As Kev1n watched, however, an expression flickered across Newt's face. A look of fear.

Kev1n tried to stop it, but it was no use. In an instant, he felt sorry for Newt Lizzard.

"Two men busted in here," Newt lisped sadly in his deaf robot voice, "and they . . . they took my dad."

"Your dad?" BB spun around, lowering his camera. "But I thought . . . Isn't he off doing that race, the one across the Gobi Desert?"

"No, no, no," Newt answered. "That was last week. He was actually here this morning. And then these guys came. They were wearing masks, I couldn't get a good look at them, but they . . . Look, I'll tell you the whole story. Just get me out of these first."

Kev1n mulled this over. "Your dad's been kidnapped—*and you call us*? Listen, Newt, if this is some ploy to get us to come over and hang out with you, you might as well—"

"Ne-hehe-he-hehe," Newt laughed. The sound resembled a donkey braying. "You think I would do all this to get you guys to hang out with me? Trust me. You are not *that* cool."

Kev1n leaned over and whispered to Monica, "Maybe you're right. Maybe he's *not* human."

Monica snickered in response.

"Look, people!" Newt rattled his cuffs. "I'd like to get

these off sometime this century! And get something to eat before I *starve to death*!"

Kev1n relaxed in his chair. He stretched out his legs, crossed his arms, and toed aside a few enormous pieces of table glass. "I calculate at least a year before you starve to death."

Monica tilted her head to consider. "Two years," she seconded. "Maybe three."

BB frowned. "C'mon, guys. There's no reason to torture him."

"Why didn't you call the police?" Kev1n challenged Newt. "Why call us?"

"I dialed you because . . . I was scared, is that what you want to hear? I didn't have a lot of time. I saw these thugs, and I . . . I saw the redial button on my cell and I just jumped on it."

"You hit redial?" Monica asked.

"Yes."

Kev1n frowned. "You hit *redial* and got BB? But we've been away for two weeks. That would mean you haven't called anybody else since we left."

Newt swallowed, nodded. "That's right. I . . . I don't have anyone to call *besides* BB."

Kev1n turned to look at Monica. He felt his face grow hot . . . blush red just like hers.

BB frowned again from across the room.

Without another word, Kev1n trudged off to find the lock pick.

6

NEWT'S TALE

Monica went to get Newt a sandwich. She entered the kitchen through a swinging door . . . and stared in amazement. It seemed less a home kitchen than the kind you'd find in a world-class restaurant. It had four stoves and three chopping tables, sinks and ovens of all sizes and degrees, and a walk-in freezer. A wall-mounted dry-erase board showed next week's menu, extensively detailing the six daily meals that were standard in the Lizzard household—breakfast, brunch, lunch, tea, dinner, and then something called "Pastry Hour." (During one such hour, Monica read, the following were to be served: baked Alaska, candied apples, bread pudding, caramel

butter cookies, hazelnut fudge, tiramisu, chocolate souf-
flé, pistachio gelato, peanut butter whim cake, and fresh
strawberry-rhubarb pie.)

Monica's stomach growled. She fetched some sandwich bread from one of several ornate bread boxes and
some ham from a deli counter that displayed an assort-
ment of exotic meats and cheeses. She had to look in five
different drawers before she found a butter knife, had to
open countless refrigerators before she found condiments.

When she brought out what she'd made, Kev1n had
already returned and undone Newt's handcuffs. Newt dove
at the food, shoving nearly half the sandwich into his
mouth.

"You're welcome," Monica said, though not as crossly
as before. She turned to Kev1n and tugged his elbow to
lead him across the room. "You should check out the
kitchen," she said softly. "I've never seen anything like it."

Kev1n stopped. "Really? Try his bedroom," he coun-
tered. "It's insane. It's a huge reptile room. Terrariums and
heat lamps and Gila monsters. It's like Newt sleeps in the
snake house of a zoo."

Monica shivered. "Just the thought gives me the
creeps. But I guess that explains a fire on a day like today.

This whole floor must be heated for the reptiles. While the rest of the building is air-conditioned."

"And the house just goes on and on," said Kev1n, "like a museum."

"Or a fun house," Monica added.

Across the room, Newt had already finished his sandwich. He stood there in striped trousers, not much taller than he'd been when cuffed to a chair.

"What are you guys whispering about?" he called.

"I was just saying that I like your snakes," Kev1n lied, pointing toward the passageway that led to Newt's bedroom, "and that your library must have every science book published in the last hundred years."

"Yes. It does. And every periodical."

"Um . . . why?" Kev1n asked.

Newt brayed, laughing like a donkey. "That's a stupid question. I *read* them."

"*All* of them?" Kev1n questioned.

"Of course."

BB returned then, having gone downstairs briefly to take some pictures of the hallway. "All done," he said.

Newt briskly nodded. "Good. With a program I wrote, we can compare your EXP3 pictures against some control photos. We're sure to uncover some evidence. And then we can use that evidence to find my dad—"

"Wait, wait, wait," Monica interrupted. "Newt, I understand that you were scared, so you called BB instead of the police. But we gotta call the police *now*. Kidnapping is totally their shtick."

"Yes," Newt said. "It is. And, you know, I would have agreed with you—before. But sitting in that chair for hours, unable to move, *waiting for you guys to arrive* . . . I got a lot of thinking done." He sauntered over, took up a fireplace poker, and stabbed at the logs. "First of all, we're in the midst of a huge blackout. The police have their hands full maintaining law and order—keeping the common people from rioting. They won't have time to investigate my father's disappearance no matter how important he is." He paused. "Second, I have developed a rather solid theory of what this is all about. And if my theory is right, involving the police might get my dad hurt."

"I don't see how getting the police involved would put your dad in *more* danger," Kev1n said.

"Yes, well, that's not surprising," Newt said dismissively.

"Newt," BB scolded.

"What? It's just that I know a lot more about the situation than he does. I'll explain." He gestured the three friends toward the upside-down sofa. They set it on its feet and sat. "I'll tell you everything, but you've got to trust me."

"Why should we?" Monica asked.

"Because I have a good idea that this involves your parents as well as mine."

"*My* parents?" Monica asked, eyeing Newt warily.

"Yes. Yours and BB's and Kev1n's mom too. All of our parents."

"That's ridiculous," Kev1n said.

Newt gave a toss of his egg-shaped head. "See if any of them are available." He pointed out the various phones around the room. He turned back to the fire and poked it some more. "Go ahead," he told them, pointing to the phones again.

Kev1n stood for a moment, then leapt up and grabbed a phone. He dialed his mom at her lab, then tried her in the loft. BB used his EXP3 to dial his dad's energy firm and the private cell numbers he had for family emergencies.

"Nothing," BB said after a few moments. "Not even answering machines."

"What about you?" Newt asked Monica. "Don't you want to try your parents?"

"I already did," she said. "And there was no answer." Her heart began to beat very fast. "And I thought at the time that it seemed highly *unusual*."

"None of this proves anything," Kev1n argued. "We're in the middle of a blackout, and nothing's how it should be. Besides, why would someone kidnap *all* our parents?"

Newt's expression was smug. "Because someone is coordinating this. Someone with a plan."

BB gasped. "That's what I've thought all along!"

"Oy vey!" Monica said. "Between the two of you, we'll be chasing UFOs before . . ." She trailed off.

She was trying hard to scoff but succeeded only in sounding even more bewildered. Something *had* been off all day. She had to admit it. And her parents not answering any of their numbers . . .

Could Newt be right?

"I suppose the conspiracy includes this blackout too? How could all of New York City losing its power have anything to do with *us*?" Her voice shook. "Impossible."

"All of *New York City*?" Newt brayed his scornful

donkey laugh. "You have no idea." Newt turned toward a blank wall, the only one bare of light fixtures and oil portraits. Facing that wall, Newt said, "Television." The wall suddenly switched on, becoming an enormous plasma screen.

"Whoa," breathed Kev1n. "Cool."

Newt barked a series of channels. The stations flipped again and again. No matter the program, broadcasters were reciting the same lines: "Only those with backup generators were lucky enough to escape . . . Cascading sequence of grid failures . . . Extending from eastern Michigan to southeast Canada . . . Cleveland, Detroit, Toronto, Ottawa . . . Darkening New Jersey and New England . . . A thin ribbon of high-voltage lines connecting southeastern New York . . . Doubt anyone in the area can even watch this now . . . Fifty million people without lights . . ."

"Wow," BB said. "It's everywhere."

"Yeah," Monica said, relieved to learn that the blackout was entirely too big to have anything to do with her. "Seems your conspirators have gone a bit overboard."

"That's what I'm telling you," Newt went on flatly. He pointed the fireplace poker at the wall-size TV for emphasis.

"We're in the middle of the biggest power failure in history. *And it has everything to do with the four of us.*"

Monica stared at Newt, letting his words sink in. Had *all* their parents been kidnapped? And had she, BB, and Kev1n been spared a Newt-style roughing up simply because they were away at camp?

"Okay, wait," BB said to his friends. "I think I see where Newt is going with this."

"You do?" Monica asked.

"Great," Kev1n said. "Start explaining. I have no idea what this kid is saying."

"Okay," BB began. "This is a massive power failure. My dad is the CEO of an energy company. Kev1n, your mom is a scientist specializing in power generation. And Monica, your parents work for Department of Environmental Protection—a government agency that deals with the energy industry. Isn't it weird that all our parents have high-level jobs dealing with power—and that they're all missing *during a blackout*?"

"Precisely," Newt droned.

Kev1n shook his head. "No. No way. It makes sense that *our* parents, mine and Monica's and BB's, would be

kidnapped because of their jobs, but *Newt's* dad is a bazil-
lionaire. He has nothing to do with this!"

He turned to Newt, who was frowning. *"Your dad*
doesn't even have a job."

"What an utterly predictable thing to say," Newt told
him. "As if being a billionaire isn't a *job!* Do you have any
idea how much money my father has? What do you think
someone does with that much money?"

"He serves his son a dozen different desserts every
night," Monica whispered, "until that son can't help but
turn into a chubby little *khazer*."

"Mon!" BB scolded.

"Sorry," Monica apologized. "So what *does* he do with
the money?"

"He invests it," Newt said, unbothered by the insult.
"My father, in particular, invests heavily in the energy
industry because, like real estate, energy tends to become
more and more scarce. Which is the same as saying more
and more valuable. Did you know my father owns control-
ling interests in the companies for which BB's parents
work?" Newt paused to make sure they understood. He
then continued, "Kidnapping a bunch of employees is fine,
but if you want to go *big time*, you're going to have to get

your hands on a stockholder—otherwise known as my dad—otherwise known as the *boss*."

"Incredible!" BB said, his eyes wide. "This *is* a conspiracy!"

Monica gave him a harsh glare. "Have I ever explained to you the meaning of *nebekh*? If you looked it up in a Yiddish dictionary, your picture would be next to it. You have clearly been watching too many movies."

"Listen, you guys," Kev1n cut in, clearly shaken. "I have no idea where my mother is. She may have been *kidnapped*, and we're just standing here. We have to do something!"

He looked at Newt. "The question is, *what* do we do? Like you said, you had a lot of time to think before we got here. I'd be very surprised if you didn't already have some kind of plan."

"Plan? Me?" Newt tried his best to look modest. Monica thought it was an emotion that didn't suit him at all. "No. No plan," Newt continued. "But I do have a good idea where we should start."

They all stared at him.

"Follow me, please."

7

NEWT'S TOAD

BB knew right where Newt was leading them: his technology room. On the various tables were printers, scanners, joysticks, and dozens of desktop computers that had been taken apart and put back together in interesting ways. Around the room there were also a half-dozen flat-screen monitors.

BB had been in the room before, during his study sessions with Newt, but it was Kev1n and Monica's first time. BB could see them gawking. Admittedly, the computer setup looked more like something you'd find in a research facility than adjoined to a twelve-year-old's bedroom. It made even BB's souped-up PC at home look puny.

Newt sat down at one of the desks and began typing away at a keyboard. For a few seconds they all waited, listening to the dozens of hard drives buzz in the background. Then a face appeared across every monitor in the room. A digitized face that, oddly enough, looked a lot like Newt. Except the electronic version was considerably slimmer.

"Wow," BB exclaimed. "I had no idea you actually had this online."

"This?" Monica asked. "What *is* this?"

"It's complicated," Newt answered, grinning ear to ear. "I think I'll let him explain." He looked at the image on the monitor closest to him and said, "TOAD, please explain what you are."

At first nothing happened. BB, who knew what an inspired programmer Newt could be, figured the program was pondering the question.

Then, in a voice that sounded only slightly more robotic than Newt's, the device spoke. "Hello, my name is TOAD, which is an abbreviation for Twinned Online Animated Device. I am an audiological proactive program whose output is channeled through a simulated visage."

Monica and Kev1n stared, mouths agape.

TOAD continued, "In common language, I am a face on a screen that can listen to what you say, think about it, and respond by talking to you. Very much like any human being, only I am, so to speak, trapped in a computer."

Monica whispered to BB, "Something about that golem's voice sounds strangely familiar."

"Kinda like one of those computerized phone operators?" BB suggested.

"Maybe," Monica started to say, "but—"

"As I was saying," the computer interrupted. "I am trapped in a computer but very aware of what is going on around me. I can both hear and see, think and respond."

"Think?" asked Kev1n. "Like a human being thinks?"

"Why not?" asked Newt. "Aren't humans just carbon-based machines? Do you really think the network that makes up your brain is so different from what's inside a cutting-edge computer?"

"Yeah," BB chimed in, "I've played plenty of video games where it seemed like the computer was thinking, trying to figure out what I'd do next, plan ahead to counter my move so the computer-generated bad guy could blow me to bits. I mean, that's a kind of intelligence, right? Predicting what will happen in the future?"

Monica shook her head in disgust. "So what? *Thinking* is easy. It's *feeling* that counts. I mean, he might be able to tell the difference between Mozart and Bach, but would either one make him *feel* anything? There are already computer programs that mimic musical instruments. You just feed them a score and they play it without having to practice or anything. But you know what? The music is terrible. Nobody wants to hear it because it lacks *feeling!*"

"Feeling?" the machine asked. "Are you suggesting I do not have feelings?"

"Well, has a good movie ever brought you to tears?" Monica asked. "Or a piano concerto made your arms tingle?"

"My arms . . . ?" the computer began.

"Or something more basic," Kev1n added. "Could you enjoy an ice cream cone? Even monkeys like ice cream, but a computer—"

"Ice cream?" the machine interjected. "I have always wanted to try ice cream. It is my dream that one day soon I will escape these confines and—"

"That's enough," Newt said. "We don't have time for these kinds of discussions. I have something I need TOAD to do." Newt asked for BB's phone. He plugged it into one of the terminals beside the keyboard. "TOAD," he said, "I want you to show us the pictures on this camera, the ones BB took earlier inside the house."

The digital head on the monitors nodded and then vanished—replaced by a picture of Kev1n and Monica holding their bikes in the train station earlier.

"That seems like forever ago," Monica said.

"Can you please concentrate?" Newt barked as a new picture cycled across the screen. Then another.

"Nothing here," Kev1n said. Then BB's picture of the cruise ship on the Hudson River scrolled up. Kev1n moved closer to one of the monitors.

"TOAD, show me the picture BB took of the dining room earlier," Newt commanded.

The picture of the cruise ship vanished and a photo of the wrecked dining room appeared.

"I don't see anything," said BB.

"Me either," answered Kev1n. "Can we go back to the cruise ship for a second?"

"Kev1n," Newt said, almost compassionately, "your

mother is in danger. Do you really think it's a good idea to waste time looking at cruise ships on the Hudson when we could actually be investigating the scene of the crime?"

"No," Kev1n answered. "I guess not."

"That's what I thought." Newt nodded. "TOAD, check your drive for a picture taken of the dining room *before* the intrusion today. Now, superimpose that image on top of the picture BB took."

Two pictures appeared on the screen, one of a very beautiful dining room and the other of the same room after it had been ransacked by the kidnappers. Slowly the two pictures began merging into one. BB was becoming more and more impressed with Newt's programming ability. He had spent a lot of hours tutoring him, but clearly the boy had been doing some studying on his own as well.

"Now," Newt told TOAD, "I want you to erase all the objects that appear in both photos, everything but the walls and floor. That way we'll at least know if the kidnappers left anything behind."

All of the furniture, pictures, and decorative trinkets began disappearing until nothing remained but a vase that, because of the superimposed photos, was both standing in the corner in one piece and shattered all over the floor. When the two vases vanished, a single object remained in a corner.

Everyone raced out of the computer lab in the direction of the dining room. They had to find out what the mysterious object was! Kev1n arrived first. By the time BB got there, he was already holding the object in his hand.

"What is it?" Monica asked.

"It's . . . it's my mother's pocket protector," Kev1n told her.

"How do you know it's your mother's?" BB asked.

"Look." Kev1n held out the protector. "It's purple, see? And it has flowers on it. It's one of a kind. She calls it her 'signature item.' She always keeps it in her lab coat. And she *always* keeps her lab coat in her laboratory downtown."

Kev1n looked frantically at his three companions. "Why is it here? Why would my mother's pocket protector be in *Newt Lizzard's* living room?"

BB opened his mouth, but nothing came out. All he could think was that the answer was obvious.

Kev1n's mom's pocket protector was here because Newt was right. It wasn't just his dad who was in trouble. It was *all* of their parents.

Kev1n stood silent, then bolted from the room. The others heard the front door slam, and when they looked out the window facing the front of the house, they saw Kev1n racing away on his bicycle.

8

THE PHANTOM CELEBRITIES

BB supposed they had no choice but to follow Kev1n downtown to his mother's lab, all the way downtown in Tribeca. Newt went to his room and brought back four wrist-mounted walkie-talkies.

"Vid-pods," he explained to Monica and BB. "I think we'll find them very useful. They'll let us see and talk to each other if we get separated for some reason. Plus they're linked to TOAD, just in case we need a little extra brainpower for our adventure."

"Um, are those going to work?" BB asked. "With the blackout and all?"

"Sure," Newt answered. "They send radio signals back

and forth to each other, kind of like walkie-talkies. And so long as we stay in the city, they'll reach back to Lizzard Mansion and TOAD too."

"Boys and their toys," Monica said glumly. "I don't suppose I have a choice of colors?"

"Sure," Newt answered. "I have this pink one and a pastel blue."

"Um, no thanks," she answered. "I'll stick with plain black."

They went outside. Even though dusk was falling, it was still incredibly hot. *And strange,* BB thought.

Normally, at this time of day, the lights in the city flickered to life. This evening there were no streetlamps, no multicolored floodlights at the top of the Empire State Building. Nothing other than the slight stink of trash starting to sour.

We might as well be back at Pine Rock Mountain, BB thought, where nightfall was always pitch-black.

"Let's catch a bus," Monica suggested. "Tribeca is a long way off."

"No way," BB told her. "Without traffic lights, the streets will be a nightmare. Even if the buses are running, it'll take us hours to get downtown."

"Great." She placed her hands on her hips. "Eighty blocks in the sweltering heat. I can't imagine anything I'd like to do less."

"Oh, come on, Monica," Newt said. "Don't be such a kvetch."

Monica gasped. "Oh no, you didn't! Yiddish is *my* thing."

"I think he *did*," BB broke in. "Besides, if Newt can handle the ride, so can you."

"Um, right," Newt said. He disappeared into a little garage by the side of the house. When he returned, he was on a Segway, a battery-powered motor scooter.

"I don't suppose you have two of those?" Monica asked him.

Newt shrugged. "Sorry."

The three of them began making their way downtown. They wove in and out of the traffic, staying away from the sidewalks, which were increasingly packed with pedestrians. BB had to remind himself that no one's televisions or computers were working. They would have no other way to find out the news than word of mouth.

We're in the Stone Age, he thought.

"So, how much ransom do you think the kidnappers will ask for?" BB asked Newt.

"Ransom?" Newt answered. "I think a lot more than ransom money is at stake."

"What do you mean?" Monica's voice echoed from the vid-pod.

BB glanced down and saw a miniaturized Monica on his wrist. Newt's vid-pods were communicating perfectly.

"Well," Newt said, "you know that Kev1n's mom, Dr. Park, is involved in some very high-end, cutting-edge research. Research that promises to radically change the world by introducing what those in the field are calling 'organic metal.'"

"Organic metal?" Monica interrupted, panting into her vid-pod. "What's that?"

"Dr. Park, one of the top metallurgists in the world, invented a special kind of steel that has a cellular memory just like living tissues," Newt explained. "It can form and re-form without the need for heat or lubricants, bending and flexing with the suppleness of a human joint—virtually eliminating the need for moving parts."

"Which everyone knows," BB added, "are the parts most likely to break."

Newt nodded. "So far she's only been able to produce tiny amounts of it because it requires an enormous amount of energy. In fact, if you could somehow harness the energy lost during today's blackout, you'd probably be able to produce about fifty pounds of it. Just enough, let's say, to make one android."

"Speaking of androids," Monica gasped into her vid-pod, "I swear I just passed Arnold Schwarzenegger here on the street."

The two boys stopped and looked back. Monica was almost a block behind them.

"No way," BB said.

"Here, look."

A blurry picture of a bodybuilder and his girlfriend appeared on BB's vid-pod.

"Close," BB told her, "but I don't think that's him."

They waited for Monica to catch up. When they were on their way again, BB asked Newt why, exactly, he knew so much about Kev1n's mother.

"Why? Because Dr. Park's research is the most significant technological investigation since the development of the microchip. It's been written about in all the science journals."

"That's right. I forgot about your library."

"The problem is, I'm not the only person who knows about her work. Corporate raiders, scientists working for foreign governments, high-tech criminals—all of these people will be aware as well. Think about it. There's a lot of money and power at stake for the person who can perfect the process, whether through legal means or not."

"I guess you're right," BB answered. "But if it's Dr. Park's research these people are after, then why kidnap *all* of our parents?"

"That's a great question," Newt answered. "I don't know the answer. But maybe when we catch up with Kev1n, we'll have more clues to work with. In the meantime, we better hurry. He might need our help."

Newt tilted his Segway forward, BB peddled faster, and Monica did her best to keep up. Every few minutes she'd see another phantom celebrity and radio the information to Newt and BB.

"I think the heat is affecting your brain," BB told her.

"Listen, I have to occupy my brain somehow," Monica huffed. "And besides, it's New York and no one has air-conditioning. I bet there are a million celebrities out on the streets tonight. So keep your eyes peeled."

"Fine, just hurry up," BB told her. He stopped and looked back, but he could no longer see her in the crowd.

A moment later she came over the radio. "Oh no!"

"What is it?" BB asked. "Did you spot Regis Philbin and Kelly Ripa?"

"No. My bike is broken. *Again.*"

"What's wrong with it?" BB asked.

"How should I know? You expect me to be able to play violin with the best orchestras in the world *and* fix a bicycle?"

Moments later BB found Monica. She was standing next to a group of kids playing in an open fire hydrant.

"It's your chain," BB told her once they had walked a short distance away from the hydrant. "It's popped off again, only this time it actually snapped. I'll call Newt and we'll find somebody to fix it. Maybe it won't take too long."

"No. Kev1n might need your help," Monica answered. "I'll get it fixed on my own and catch up with you."

"Are you sure?"

"Yes. Besides, I need a rest from pedaling."

BB started to radio Newt that he was coming back, but Monica placed her hand on his arm, stopping him.

"BB? Be careful," she said.

BB smirked. "You mean more careful than I would normally be chasing after a bunch of parent-nappers, who might also have cut off half the country's electricity?"

"Yes, more careful than that," she said. "I've been thinking, and something about Newt's story just doesn't add up."

"Really?" BB asked. "What?"

"The fire in the fireplace," Monica told him. "If Newt was handcuffed to the chair for six hours, who exactly was tending the fire?"

"Maybe Newt's dad put a lot of wood in there before he got kidnapped," BB guessed.

"Maybe," Monica allowed. "But there's more. That bounce back I heard on the phones earlier? I think I heard it behind TOAD's voice. And for that matter, I hear it when we use these vid-pods too."

"Now who's being paranoid?" BB asked.

Monica shook her head. "I know. It sounds weird, but—"

"But nothing," BB said. "You and Kev1n are my best friends, but this whole hangup you two have about Newt is starting to wear thin. Especially when it seems to me that all four of us are in exactly the same boat. *All* of our parents seem to be missing, and we're *all* upset."

"You're right," Monica answered. "And I'm sorry. But you should still be careful, okay?"

"Don't worry," BB assured her. "I will. And you should too. Radio us as soon as you get your bike fixed. And no more celebrity sightings!"

"Well, I won't make any promises." Monica smiled. "It's like a sweatier version of the Oscars out here. Look! There are the Olsen twins."

"Cool. Ask them if they know how to fix your chain."

9

ANKARA BRACELING

When Ankara Braceling crawled out of bed on the evening of the blackout, she was so groggy she could barely open her eyes. At the same time, there was something going on in her stomach—something warning her that she'd better find the bathroom right away.

These are the problems with being an old woman, she thought. *Never knowing when you're going to fall asleep and now—*

Her stomach made an awful sound. She began walking faster down the hallway, trying her best to keep her eyes open.

Not that she needed her eyes open. She *could* have

found her way around Lizzard Mansion in her sleep. She knew every nook and cranny of that huge house because *Newt* knew every nook and cranny too.

Keeping up with Newt Lizzard was Ankara's primary responsibility. You might say it was also her passion.

She walked down the hallway, then stopped suddenly. Something in the house wasn't right.

After all these years, Ankara had developed a sixth sense about Newt's presence and well-being. Right now that sense was telling her that Newt wasn't in the house. And worse, he was either *in* some kind of trouble or about to *cause* some kind of trouble. She couldn't always tell the difference.

This ability of hers often struck Newt as bizarre. Sometimes she'd yell at him from two rooms away telling him to stop, for example, playing with an expensive antique.

Once Newt went so far as to ask if she were telepathic. "No," she told him, "I just make a point of paying attention. Especially when it involves *you*."

Growing up in Turkey, Ankara's keen awareness of her surroundings had often made the difference between survival and extinction.

For example, maybe somebody wanted to know what vendor had just received a shipment of Japanese televisions. Well, Ankara happened to be passing by when the workers were unloading the truck just the other day.

Or if some rich lady wanted to know where she could find the newest and coolest American jeans, Ankara inevitably had seen a woman walking out of a store not ten blocks away, wearing those very jeans. And the woman hadn't even taken the tags off yet.

Eventually Ankara decided that she was growing too old to be traveling in such circles, leading shady characters around the ancient city's back streets. So she turned her knowledge into a job as a guide for the many tourists visiting Turkey. It was a good living, especially when the Americans, who tipped well, visited.

Then one day, about twelve years ago, she was sitting in a coffee shop when she overheard a man talking on his cell phone. The man, Reginald Lizzard, had come to Turkey to buy some very valuable and very ancient artifacts. It seemed that his connection in Turkey had vanished and the person who was actually in possession of the artifacts couldn't be found. When the man got off the phone, Ankara went over to his table and said, "The man you're looking for, I've heard his name. I bet I could find him for you. In fact, I bet I could find anybody you were looking for in all of Turkey."

Reginald Lizzard, always an excellent judge of character, hired Ankara on the spot. For the next week, she led him around the city as he collected the expensive artifacts.

At the end of the week, he received a telegram explaining that he should come back home because he was the father of twins, a boy and a girl. Reginald, who had been incredibly impressed with Ankara, asked her to return to New York with him and be his children's nanny. Any woman who could handle herself on the back streets of Turkey would have no trouble keeping up with a couple of kids. Ankara agreed.

When Reginald and his wife divorced and Sally went with her mother, Ankara stayed with Newt and his father.

"Finder's keepers," Reginald told his wife. "Go to Turkey and find your own super-nanny."

And now where is that boy? Ankara asked herself as she made her way down the hallway.

He might just be taking one of his naps. . . .

But then *why* did she have this funny feeling?

When she reached the dining room, she understood why. The place was in a shambles!

Ankara called for Newt, worried. Before long, she noticed the handcuffs on the floor and *really* began to worry. She raced to Newt's room and began searching for clues. She pulled open his sock drawer—and the first thing she found was a bottle of sleeping pills.

Is this why I fell asleep right after my morning tea? Ankara wondered. She took a deep breath. Chances were, the answer was *yes*.

Ankara frowned deeply. *That boy,* she thought. *If he's not in serious trouble already, he is going to be when I find him!*

10
THE MYSTERIOUS POCKET PROTECTOR

When Newt and BB arrived at the lab in Tribeca, BB spotted Kev1n's bike. It was leaning against the side of the building, unlocked and completely vulnerable. BB was amazed that it hadn't been stolen. He grabbed the bike by the handlebars, then stepped up to the front door and knocked. No one answered.

"Ring the buzzer," Newt suggested.

"But it's not going to work," BB answered. "There's no power."

"I'm sure there is," Newt told him. "A lab like this is bound to have a backup generator. Otherwise they'd risk losing valuable work every time the electricity went out."

BB pressed the button and discovered that Newt was right. The buzzer could be heard going off somewhere inside the building.

"What took you so long?" Kev1n's voice asked through the speaker.

"Traffic," BB answered. "Did you find your mom?"

"No. She's not here. Hold on and I'll buzz you guys up."

BB and Newt pulled both bicycles and the Segway into the foyer, then joined Kev1n in the lab.

"Hey! Where's Mon?" Kev1n asked as they walked through the door.

BB explained that Monica's bike chain had broken again, then he looked around. To him, the lab seemed completely in order. All the equipment glistened under the halogen lamps, and the floor looked so clean you could eat off it. Not a single thing was out of place.

"Is that your mom's lab coat hanging on the door?" BB asked.

"Yes," Kev1n answered. "Right where she always leaves it anytime she's not actually wearing it. And there's something else. Her pocket protector is still in there."

"What?" BB asked. "How is that possible?" He went

over to the coat to check for himself. Sure enough, there was a purple flowered protector in its pocket.

"Does she have two of these?" BB asked.

"No," Kev1n answered. "She has *one*. The one in her coat pocket hanging on the door."

Newt walked around the lab, greedily inspecting the equipment. "*That* pocket protector could be a decoy," Newt suggested. "The kidnappers could have put it there in case anyone stopped by. That way, no one would think anything was wrong."

"A decoy? No," Kev1n said. "This pocket protector is the *real* pocket protector. It has my mom's name written on the inside."

BB glanced inside the lab coat's pocket. Sure enough, there was Kev1n's mom's name, rendered in swirly purple ink.

"I forgot that little detail till I got here," Kev1n continued. "The pocket protector I saw at your house? It didn't have her name on it, and that leaves me with two questions. First, why was there a fake pocket protector on your floor? And second, where is my mother?"

Newt didn't respond.

"Fine," Kev1n huffed. "If you're not going help, then get out of my way."

He slid into his mother's office chair and flipped on her computer. It buzzed and whirred as it began its elaborate start-up process.

"Um, Kev? No way you're getting into that thing," BB said, looking over Kev1n's shoulder. "All those prompts it's going through? That's some seriously hack-proof code. More safeguards than Fort Knox."

"Fort Knox didn't give us much trouble," Kev1n responded. "I don't expect this to either."

BB pointed at the screen. "But look. That's military-grade security software. You type in the wrong password too many times and *poof!* No more computer to hack."

"If you're finished drooling over my mom's PC," Kev1n said, "maybe you could pass me that little box that looks like a webcam." BB handed him the box, and Kev1n put it up against his eye. He pressed the keyboard's return key.

The computer displayed a welcome message.

"You're in?" BB asked. "Just like that?"

Kev1n nodded. "There's a back door programmed to my retinal scan. My mom likes me to see the kind of work she does." He glanced at Newt, who was lingering near the door. "We're close that way."

Turning back to BB, he said, "Let's check my mom's computer log. See if anyone's attempted to access the system recently."

BB sat beside Kev1n and typed in a few commands. "No," he told Kev1n, "it doesn't look like anyone's accessed it since, well, about five o'clock yesterday."

"That means my mom didn't even show up for work this morning!" Kev1n yelped.

"Of course not," Newt said, still lingering near the door. "I keep telling you, it's because she was too busy being kidnapped."

"I'm not so sure," Kev1n said. "And there's something else I want to check out. BB, plug the EXP3 in here."

BB did as Kev1n asked.

"Those pictures you took. There was something funny in one of them. . . ." Kev1n scrolled through the photos and stopped at the one of the cruise ship sailing up the Hudson River.

"Zoom." He pointed at part of the screen, where a group of people were standing on deck. BB zoomed in on the area.

"More," Kev1n said. The viewfinder swooped in, and the image slowly resolved.

"There!" Kev1n shouted. "I knew it!"

In the picture, BB could make out the face of—Kev1n's mom! She was on board the ship, standing alongside—BB blinked—alongside his own parents! And Monica's too!

All five of them were laughing and clearly having a good time.

"I don't understand," BB said. "If they were on that boat earlier today—"

"Then they weren't kidnapped," Kev1n cut in. "I don't understand it either, but maybe *Newt* can explain. Since he's so full of answers today."

The two boys spun toward Newt. He was standing directly behind them now, a knowing grin spread across his face. In his hand, Newt held something that resembled a large remote control. He pointed it at BB.

"Hey, what are you doing?" BB asked.

"What I am doing," Newt returned, his deaf robot voice more grating than ever, "is holding a laser blaster—a little something I had especially manufactured by one of my dad's companies. It may not look like much, but I assure you, it packs a powerful punch."

He pointed the blaster at Dr. Park's lab coat and fired. Immediately the coat burst into flames.

Kev1n balled his hands into fists. His shoulders shook with rage. "I gave my mom that coat for Christmas," he said, standing up and taking a step toward the pudgy villain.

"Yes, this blaster really does a job on cotton fiber," Newt observed. "Want to see what it does to *human skin*?"

He pointed the blaster at Kev1n, who came to an abrupt halt.

"I didn't think so." Newt switched the blaster to his opposite hand. "Let's cut to the chase. I suppose the least I can do now is give you some sort of explanation as to what's been going on today. I can see that you're both confused."

"That would be awfully nice of you," Kev1n grumbled, gritting his teeth.

"As you have already surmised, the kidnappings were nothing more than a ruse. A brilliant bit of misdirection, but a ruse just the same. Earlier this week, Kev1n, your mother received a phone call from a travel company informing her that she had been chosen for a surprise vacation starting today. For reasons I will get into in a moment, I wanted her out of the way. I had no idea that she would invite BB's and Monica's parents along. I learned about it only this morning. But it is summer in New York. It's no surprise that they would jump at the opportunity to escape the city for a few days."

Newt paused and then added, "Guess who owns the travel company."

BB sighed. "Is there anything your father *doesn't* own?"

"Yes, in fact. He *doesn't* own six of the seven major energy companies in the eastern United States and Canada. But with BB's help, during our little study sessions, I've been able to break into all of their mainframes and derail the electrical conduits that deliver power to the East Coast. That is, I was able to cause the largest blackout in U.S. history. Pretty impressive, if I do say so myself."

"What?" Kev1n asked, turning to BB. "You broke into all those companies—for *this* guy?"

"N-no way," BB objected. "I didn't break into anything."

"No," Newt explained, "you didn't. But you did teach me the skills I needed to do it myself. I've always been able to program, but hacking was not my specialty. Thanks to you, I can now channel the power from all those companies into a facility my father *does* own, a little warehouse I've specially outfitted. . . .

"But I'm saying too much too quickly. The two of you won't need to know where this warehouse is because you won't be tagging along."

"Great," Kev1n said. "I was right. Newt *is* an evil genius."

A look of disappointment crossed BB's face. "But Newt, why? What are you going to do with all this power? And why did you need to involve us?"

"I was getting to that. Another thing my father does not own is the company for which Kev1n's mother works. Now that he has conveniently unlocked this unhackable computer, I'll be able to copy her process for creating organic metal. With it and Dr. Park's smelting device, I'll be able to manufacture enough organic metal to produce a real live body."

"For what?" BB asked.

"Why, for TOAD, of course!" Newt giggled.

"What?" BB and Kev1n exclaimed in unison.

"He'll be an android. But a kind of android we could previously only dream of," Newt explained. "Not only will his organic metal skin make him indestructible and stronger than any human could ever be, but with my programming, he will be the perfect friend."

He placed a sympathetic hand on BB's shoulder. "Not that the two of you and Monica aren't nice. It's just that really, there's no substitute for good technology."

"There's no way we're going to help you," Kev1n grumbled.

"No, I didn't think you would. All you need to do is hang out until everything is finished. That way you'll be out of harm's way. And out of *my* way."

"Very considerate of you," Kev1n said. "I suppose by 'hang out' you mean 'stay locked up somewhere.'"

"Imagine, all this time I thought BB and Monica were the smart ones," Newt joked. "Yes, Kev1n, that is exactly what I mean. And that closet there will do just fine."

He marched forward, pointing the laser at Kev1n's chest. "Please, won't you step inside?"

For a moment, Kev1n didn't move.

"Newt," BB said softly. "Don't do this. I told Kev1n and Monica you weren't a bad guy. I—I believed in you."

For a moment, Newt's features softened. Then he

shrugged. "Sorry. Guess you won't make that mistake again."

Newt forced the two boys into the closet, closed the door, and pointed his laser blaster at the lock. He pushed the button. A beam of light shot from the end. The metal door knob turned red, then bubbled and melted, making it impossible for BB and Kev1n to escape.

Newt stood there, reveling in his excellent work. Then he realized—he had locked the boys in the closet with BB's wrist-mounted vid-pod!

Oh no, Newt thought. *Now they'll be able to warn Monica!*

A second later, he chuckled to himself. Perhaps that wasn't such a bad thing after all. As soon as Monica arrived, Newt would have the final ingredient he needed to put his plan into action. TOAD would be incarnated in a *real live body*. And Newt would have a real live super-intelligent, super-strong friend.

He shuffled over to Dr. Park's computer and down-loaded the formula he needed for the organic metal. He took the high-tech smelting device that would actually do the work, strapped it to his Segway, and began making his way toward the warehouse in Queens, where five tons of raw ore waited.

Newt laughed long and loud. He could hardly contain his excitement.

AN IMPROMPTU CARNIVAL

I t didn't take Ankara Braceling very long to figure out what Newt was up to. The boy kept extensive notes on whatever crazy idea he happened to be cooking up.

Not that Newt was careless with those notes.

No, his father had bought him an authentic World War II encoding manual for his birthday some years back, which Newt had studied and memorized. Between that and his terrible handwriting, the CIA would have had trouble unraveling his plans.

But Ankara wasn't paid to be baffled by Newt Lizzard. She was paid to stay one step ahead of him.

She discovered the coded notebook between Newt's

mattresses, spent a few minutes decoding it, then grabbed her purse and rushed out the door.

Before she reached the street, she already knew the city was in a blackout. Newt's notebook had explained as much. But when she got outside, she realized *exactly* what that meant. The streets were full of people who had fled their sweltering apartments and were quickly turning New York into a gigantic carnival.

On the stoop of one of the nearby stores, a couple of men were holding bongos between their knees and drumming on them. It was a Caribbean rhythm that reminded Ankara of the annual Puerto Rican Day Parade.

On the opposite corner, a group of kids took turns jumping through a fire hydrant exploding with water. Somewhere farther away, a car stereo boomed and rattled the windows of the other cars parked on the street.

This just won't do, Ankara thought. She wouldn't be able to find a bus or a taxi in this traffic, and the subways wouldn't be running at all. She could walk, but at the speed she moved, everything would be over by the time she arrived.

Then she remembered—the four-wheeled scooter Reginald Lizzard had bought to celebrate her ten-year anniversary with the family. For years he had listened to her complain about her aching bones. He thought that the motor-powered scooter would help her get around. But Ankara had too much pride to ride around the city on one of those devices. It made her look like an old woman!

Granted, she was beginning to *feel* like an old woman, but that didn't mean she had to *look* like one.

Now the scooter would come in very handy indeed. She pulled it out of the garage, sat down on its seat, and began zooming downtown toward Tribeca. She yelled for street revelers to get out of her way. The moment people caught sight of her, flying down the middle of the sidewalk at a very high speed, they didn't argue.

Ankara was a few blocks away from Kev1n's mother's laboratory when she hit the brakes. There was Newt, clear as day, heading away from the building on his Segway. She started to yell for him, but the cars lined up for the Holland Tunnel were honking up a storm. By the time she crossed the street, Newt had vanished.

Where is he going? she asked herself, thinking back to the notebook. *Ah, yes. The expressway! He'll hop on and make his way to Queens. To his father's warehouse.*

Ankara hit the accelerator on her scooter. The tiny vehicle hit a curb—and stopped dead in its tracks. She was stuck. She pressed the pedal again, then tried putting it in reverse. Still the scooter wouldn't move.

"You see," she complained to a pedestrian passing nearby, "I *am* an old woman. Only an old woman could possibly get her scooter stuck in the middle of a blackout."

And, she added silently to herself, *only a boy like Newt would have his poor nanny out on this night, chasing him all over the city.*

Newt smiled. All around him, the darkened streets were eerily lit by flashlights, flares, and candles. People were sitting on their stoops listening to battery-powered radios. Some were tuning to the news, trying to find out when the electricity might be restored. Others were listening to music instead, the people around them dancing in the streets.

Single-handedly *he* had caused New York (and half of the rest of the country) to mutate into a tremendous outdoor party. It might have been the Fourth of July, only darker and without the fireworks.

When all this is over, he thought, *people should thank*

me. In fact, they should give me some kind of a medal!

As he neared the Queensboro Bridge, Newt's thoughts turned to his brilliant plan. He wondered once more if it would all unfold as he hoped.

Yes! he told himself. *It's going to work perfectly! And tomorrow TOAD will be real!*

So what if Monica Steen had to be terminated to make it happen?

12

ON THE ROAD AGAIN

After her chain broke, Monica remembered a bike shop just a few blocks away. She had passed by it many times with her parents, on their way out of the city to visit Aunt Margaret and Uncle Abe.

The old couple were sweet, but as soon as they learned of Monica's musical ability, they insisted she learn a bunch of old folk songs—and play them every time she visited.

Monica pushed her bike the few blocks to the shop, but when she arrived, she found it closed. She propped the bike against the fence and sat on the curb, unsure of what to do next. Should she just push her bike down to Tribeca? Kev1n would probably be able to fix the chain.

Still, she thought, *that's a long walk in this heat.* Just as she began to lose herself in indecision, someone spoke to her.

"Looks to me," the man said, "like you're having a mechanical emergency."

"Why is it," Monica asked, without looking up, "that a bicycle shop would close just because there's a blackout? Seems to me like the lack of electricity would make bicycles *more* valuable."

"I think everybody just enjoys having a day off—especially an unexpected day off," the man answered.

Monica looked up at the man—and immediately recognized him. An honest-to-goodness celebrity!

"Oh my gosh!" she exclaimed.

This man—the man in front of her—had a show on one of the cable channels, where he took pieces from old, run-down machines and turned them into the most incredible inventions. She specifically recalled an episode where he took a ceiling fan, a skateboard, a bedsheet and the solar cells off two dozen handheld calculators and made a really cool street-surfing thingamabob.

It was Kev1n's favorite show. Now if only Monica could remember his name . . .

The man pulled a pair of pliers out of his backpack and straightened his thick-rimmed glasses. "Mind if I have a look?"

"By all means." Monica beamed.

Within minutes, he had the bicycle chain fixed.

"Th-thanks," Monica stuttered, still a little starstruck.

"Nothing to it. What else am I going to do during a blackout but help a nice young lady out of her troubles?"

She thanked the man again and explained that she had to be going, that she was late to meet up with her friends.

"You be careful," the celebrity told her. Then, as she was getting on her bike, he asked, "By the way, you're Monica Steen, right? The violin player?"

"You know who I am?" she asked.

"Do I ever. I've got a recording of your Tel Aviv concert and I listen to it all the time. I'm trying to get my producer to use it as the theme song for my show!"

Monica grinned. It hadn't occurred to her that *she* might be one of the many celebrities out on the street today.

"Wow," she said. "Thanks so much for your help. If you want to use my music for your show, just call my agent. I'll give it to you for free. At this point, I owe you one anyway."

She waved goodbye and began bicycling downtown. After a block or two, she radioed BB. "Hey! My bike is fixed! And guess who I just met."

"Who?" BB asked. "Santa Claus or the Easter Bunny?"

"Better than both. The guy from the show Kev1n likes so much, the one where the guy builds all the thingies."

"You're lying!" Kev1n and BB yelled into BB's vid-pod.

"Nope. I swear."

"Um, Mon, that's totally cool," BB continued, "but we have news of our own."

BB began explaining everything they had discovered in the last hour—the fact that the kidnappings were fake, Newt's plan to build an android, and how he had stolen the formulas from Dr. Park's laboratory and locked him and Kev1n in the closet.

"Feh," Monica said. "So he's going to build some kind of living robot? Who cares? I'll come down there and break you guys out and then we'll finally enjoy our escape from Pine Rock Mountain."

BB's voice came over the radio. "You don't understand, Monica. I've been doing some calculations. If Newt funnels all the downed power to his dad's one plant, well, he'll cause a *massive* overload. Transformers will blow up all over the city. And by blow up, I mean like bombs. *Kaboom!* Lives are at stake. We've got to stop him."

"*We* have to stop him? What are we? Superheroes or something?"

"Or something," BB echoed.

"Just an idea," Monica said, "but maybe it's time we involve the police?"

"Sure, you do that," Kev1n said. "Go tell the police that a twelve-year-old kid is behind the largest blackout in history. Not only that, but this kid is planning to use all that stolen electricity to create a robotic best friend. By the time you're done with the psychiatric evaluation, the whole island will be up in smoke."

"He's right, Monica," BB joined in. "I think we're on our own here."

Monica sighed. "Okay, I'll come get you guys out. The Blackout Gang will be reunited and we'll save the world from Newt."

"The Blackout Gang? That's good," Kev1n said. "But I have more bad news. There's no way you're getting into this lab to break us out. Other than my mom and her assistants, I'm the only person who can open the front door. Until BB and I find a way to break ourselves out, you're going to have to deal with Newt on your own."

"Ugh!"

"Come on, Mon," BB sweet-talked. "You're not the kind of girl to let an evil genius with a Napoleon complex get you down. You'll be fine."

Monica was just beginning to blush at the compliment when BB spoke up again. "Hold on. I'll find out where the little mad scientist went."

Monica parked her bike on the corner and waited as BB worked his way through the firewalls on his vid-pod.

"Okay, I've hacked past TOAD's first lines of defense. I'm online," BB said. He tapped a few more buttons on the vid-pod. "This is it. Newt's father owns one warehouse in the metro area. It's in Queens. I'm getting you the plans for the whole place. Check them out. You shouldn't have any trouble getting in and sneaking up on Newt."

Monica looked at the blueprints BB had sent her and decided that it *would* be easy to break in on Newt. Too easy.

Could it be some kind of trap?

It didn't matter. She had no choice but to go after him. She couldn't very well let entire neighborhoods go up in smoke.

She said goodbye to the boys, turned her bike around, and began heading northeast toward Queens.

She had to laugh when she passed an old woman standing beside her four-wheeled scooter, kicking it and swearing in some language Monica didn't understand.

For a minute, Monica thought about stopping and helping the old lady, but there wasn't time. Newt was already well ahead of her and she had to hurry.

By the time she made it up to 60th Street, Monica was just about sick of the blackout revelers. They all seemed to be delirious from the heat, and they were continuously bumping into her, making it very hard for her to bicycle. She crossed over to Second Avenue and saw what appeared to be a parade of some sort passing through. There were about forty people—singing, playing instruments, or holding candles—crossing right in front of her.

She got off her bicycle and tried to push it through the crowd on foot. She felt something snag on her wrist. She looked down and saw that her vid-pod was missing.

She turned to see where it had fallen. There! A few feet behind her, right in the path of the parade.

Crunch.

Monica watched as one person after another stepped on the vid-pod. When she was finally able to get into the crowd to pick it up, it had been completely destroyed.

Great, she thought. *There goes my connection to BB and Kev1n.*

She crossed the road, climbed back on her bicycle, and began making her way over the Queensboro Bridge.

From the middle of the bridge's span, she paused a moment to look at the city. It was completely dark, and from where she stood, it seemed absolutely peaceful.

Looking at it, knowing what had caused the blackout—and what would happen next if she didn't hurry—gave her the shivers.

She began pedaling again as fast as she could.

13

THE MIND OF TOAD

should not be speaking to you," TOAD told the boys in his mechanical voice.

"What, are you a chicken?" Kev1n asked.

"No, I am TOAD. A Twinned Online Animated—"

"I mean *scared*," Kev1n interrupted. "Are you scared to talk to us? Maybe you think Newt will find out and cancel his plans for making you real. Maybe instead he'll turn you into an automated toaster oven."

"Scared?" TOAD answered. "No, I know no more of fear than I do of ice cream. And now, since you insist on being rude, I will stop talking to you altogether. Have a pleasant day."

"Bah!" BB threw up his hands. "Now you've made him angry!"

"Whatever. If he can't be scared, then he can't be angry either." Kev1n paused. "Though apparently he can be difficult."

For the past half hour Kev1n and BB had been questioning TOAD via BB's vid-pod, trying their best to get information about Newt's plan.

In fact, they had gotten nowhere. Even if TOAD couldn't get angry or afraid, the two boys could.

They *had* to break out of the closet and help Monica.

"Couldn't Newt just get a puppy like everybody else?" Kev1n wondered aloud. He turned to BB. "What should we do now?"

BB tapped his lower lip. "Maybe the problem is that we've been trying to *pressure* TOAD. But he's just a computer program. Granted, a very complex program, but still a program. You can't pressure them. They just recognize and follow rules."

"What rules?" Kev1n asked.

"All sorts—mathematical, geometrical, linguistic—whatever you program into them. *Logical* rules."

"So we're supposed to *reason* with him?"

"It's worth a try."

BB began messaging TOAD, trying to get him to come back online and talk to them. When he finally told TOAD that he had something very important to tell him about Newt, the voice returned.

"I will speak to you for a moment," TOAD droned, "but I hope you are telling me the truth. I really do not like liars."

BB whispered to Kev1n, "Let me handle this. I think I know how to get him."

"Be my guest," Kev1n said. "If you need me to poke him in the eye, just let me know."

"TOAD," BB called, "you just said you hope we are telling you the truth. I think I know why you said that."

"I am listening . . ." TOAD said, "for the time being."

"If people started lying regularly, you'd never know when anyone was telling the truth. You'd never be able to trust anyone, even on the least little thing. Right?"

"That is correct," TOAD answered.

"Same with stealing," BB continued. "If it were okay for people to steal, then it would be pretty pointless for anyone to own anything since somebody would just come along and take it. Are you with me?"

"Yes, I have various texts on file that speak of these things," TOAD answered.

"Right," BB said. "But what I'm getting at is that Newt has stolen millions upon millions of megawatts of energy for his own purposes. What do you think would happen if everybody did that?"

"There would not be enough electricity to go around. Eventually there would be chaos," TOAD concluded.

"That's right. And what will happen when Newt tries to channel that energy?"

"There's a very big risk of explosions," TOAD answered.

"Yes. We're talking billions of dollars in destroyed property. What if everyone acted that way?"

"Then no property would be safe."

"And what about the *people* who will be hurt by the explosions? Even killed?" BB kept on. "What if everyone were so careless with other people's lives?"

"Then no one would be safe."

"That's right. Not even Newt." BB paused for a moment, but TOAD didn't answer. "TOAD? Are you still there?"

The boys waited. And waited.

"You've made him angry again," Kev1n complained.

"He can't *get* angry. Remember?" BB took off his baseball cap and scratched his head. "Maybe he's just thinking it over."

A few moments later TOAD's voice returned. "I apologize for the time it has taken me to respond, but I seem to be stuck in a very troublesome loop."

"A loop?" Kev1n asked. "What is he talking about?"

"He means a logical loop," BB explained.

"Yes," TOAD continued. "The problem is that I know what Newt is doing and why. He wants me to have a real body so the two of us can be real friends. As you know, Newt doesn't have any real friends. But it's not entirely selfish. He also wants mc to bc capable of enjoying life in the way hc does. And personally, I have always desired to taste a chocolate ice cream cone . . ."

TOAD trailed off for a moment, then continued. "I have decided that the things you have mentioned are not problematic. The theft of electricity is only temporary. It will be restored to normal very quickly. And the possibility of explosions and some harm to others are unpleasant consequences, but they are not intentional on Newt's part. These are concerns I have decided to ignore."

"What?" BB asked. "How can you ignore them when—"

"Allow me to finish," TOAD interrupted. "There is only one thing I am having trouble excusing, and that is the intentional destruction of your friend Monica."

"The destruction of Monica?" Kev1n yelled.

"Yes," TOAD continued. "For me to assume a life-like form, there must be a body to which the organic metal can be melded. Then my programming can be transplanted. The two processes will necessarily destroy the body's original owner. The body Newt intends to use is Monica's."

"Oh no! Get her on the phone. Get her on the phone!" Kev1n urged.

BB frantically pushed the vid-pod's buttons. "I can't reach her. She's not answering! TOAD!" BB yelled into the vid-pod.

"Yes," the machine answered.

"You have to get us out of here!"

"Yes," TOAD agreed. "I have already decided to set you free."

"You can't keep us here," BB argued. "You . . . Wait, what did you say?"

"I have decided to set you free so that you can help

your friend. As much as I want to experience the world as the two of you do, I cannot accept the intentional destruction of the girl Monica. Please move away from the door."

"What are you doing?" BB asked TOAD.

"I am tapping into the computer system in the lab," TOAD responded. "From there I will be able to control a laser mounted on a 360-degree swiveling arm. I will use that to open the door. Please clear the area," TOAD advised.

BB and Kev1n stepped away from the door, pressing their backs against the closet's far wall. A minute later, the door's hinges glowed bright red. BB and Kev1n could feel the heat against their faces.

With a loud *hiss*, the hinges melted and the door fell out of its frame.

"All right! Now we'd better hurry," BB said.

"Yeah," Kev1n answered. "You go ahead. I'll be with you in a minute." He ran from the closet and dashed to the nearest bathroom.

Before BB had made it ten blocks, Kev1n was again at his side. The two of them pedaled as quickly as they could—toward the warehouse in Queens and, hopefully, a Monica who had not yet been destroyed.

14

A MAN IN A FEZ

Ankara Braceling was in a jam.

Rather, her scooter was jammed. At first, she thought it was only stuck on the curb. But when it finally rolled back into the street, she discovered that something was wrong with the device itself. When she hit the accelerator, it would only shake and buzz.

Great, she thought. *I had counted on catching up with that boy here in Manhattan. Now he has too much of a head start!*

Ankara was a long way from Queens with no way to get there but her feet. She began mumbling to herself in Turkish.

"Hello?" A man walked up, wearing a fez.

"Do I know you?" Ankara asked, narrowing her eyes at the stranger.

"No, I haven't had the pleasure. But your accent is Turkish. I myself am from Istanbul. My name is Sener."

"Nice to meet you, Sener. I'm Ankara . . . from Ankara. I don't suppose you know how to fix these things," she said, pointing at the scooter.

"No," he told her. "But is there somewhere you need to go?"

"Yes, there is. The boy I take care of is about to cause a lot of trouble and I need to get to Queens to stop him."

"What kind of trouble, if you don't mind me asking?"

"The usual kind," she explained. "Explosions. Power outages. A young girl whose life is in danger."

"Oh my goodness," Sener said, scratching his chin. "Is that the kind of trouble children cause these days? When I was a boy in Istanbul, the worst I did was forget to wash my hands before dinner."

"Well, I don't know about all children, but it's pretty usual for Newt Lizzard," Ankara told him.

Sener smiled. "I'm sure he's a good boy at heart, Ankara from Ankara. Shall I help you get to Queens?"

"Do you have a car?"

"Better!" he answered.

The man asked Ankara to get back on the scooter and he began pushing it. His strength surprised her, especially since he couldn't be much younger than she was. He stopped outside a bike shop, the same bike shop that only twenty minutes earlier Monica had discovered closed. Sener took out his keys and opened the gate. He pushed the scooter inside and pulled out a bicycle taxi. He made a dramatic bow and invited Ankara to sit down in the carriage in the back. He himself climbed up front.

"It's a long way to Queens," Ankara told him. "Are you sure you're up for this?"

"Oh, I've been doing bicycle taxi tours since I was a small boy in Istanbul. It used to be the Hagia Sophia, the Blue Mosque, and the Topkapi Palace in the morning. In the afternoon, I covered the Hippodrome, the Grand Bazaar, and the Spice Market. New York is easy. There aren't really any hills."

"Great," she told him. "Let's get going."

Sener began pedaling and, without looking, turned into oncoming traffic.

A flood of headlights filled Ankara's cab. An ambulance was coming right at her!

"Watch out!" she gasped.

Sener swung the taxi up on two wheels, narrowly missing the speeding ambulance.

"Do not worry, Ankara from Ankara. You're in good hands," he turned around to tell her.

"I'm sure I am," Ankara panted, "but could you please keep your eyes on the road?"

Sener nodded and began weaving in and out of the traffic. All the while, he regaled Ankara with tales from his homeland.

". . . And that's when the merchant told me you couldn't buy a magic lamp with Byzantine coins!" Sener cracked himself up.

"What is that?" Ankara asked. "Some story you made up to tell the tourists?"

"Made up?" Sener laughed. "Never."

Ankara's eyes opened wide as a hot dog vendor pushed his cart right into their path.

"Watch the road!" she shouted.

Sener shrugged. "It's all under control." He swerved to avoid the vendor, then turned around again. "Ankara from Ankara, do you ever miss Turkey?"

"Yes. Everything but the bicycle taxi drivers," she

answered, gripping the sides of the cab. "And where are you going anyway?"

"The Williamsburg Bridge," Sener answered. "It's much prettier than the Queensboro, don't you think?"

With that he swung the taxi up on two wheels and made a right turn onto Delancey. Soon they were on the bridge.

"It is a nice view," Ankara agreed, looking back at the Manhattan skyline. Without any lights, the city look liked one huge, jagged mountain of rock. "A very nice view," she continued, "but I do wish you'd hurry."

"No problem," Sener stated. "I will have you in Queens in no time!"

Ankara was jerked back in her seat as Sener stood up on the pedals and raced across the bridge.

15

THE EASIEST BREAK-IN EVER

Monica arrived at the Lizzard warehouse and found the gate to the chain-link fence locked. She thought about climbing over, but when she looked up, she made out razor wire glistening in the moonlight.

Ouch, she thought. *Maybe not.*

She walked around the fence, wondering how she might get in. She remembered the plans BB had shown her well enough—like musical scores, blueprints were all about patterns. But there had been no information about the property *around* the warehouse.

She walked toward the front gate and saw a section of the fence that had been pulled up. She had begun to crawl underneath when she heard something behind her and suddenly stopped.

She turned and saw a shadow dart behind a wrecked car parked on the street.

"Who's there?" she called.

When no one answered, she shrugged and finished crawling under the fence.

The yard inside the gate was completely empty except for some wooden crates and rusted old oil drums. The security lights inside the warehouse windows were working, so the building still had power.

Of course, Monica thought. *It's the power that Newt stole. The power he needs to bring his friend to life!*

She tried to stay in the shadows, out of the beams of the security lights. Hiding behind one of the steel drums, she found the vent she had planned to climb through to get into Newt's secret lab.

Nearby, she spied a couple of empty oil containers. Monica placed a large crate on the ground under the grate, then lifted an empty drum on top of that.

There, she thought. *Just the right height.* She climbed up.

Before she knew it, she was perched inside the lightless

shaft of the vent. In front of her were dozens of ducts, heading off in a dozen different directions.

All right, she thought, *let's see how good my memory really is.*

She took a deep breath and began crawling her way carefully through the ventilation shafts. Every time she put down her hand or knee, the aluminum under her made a loud popping sound. She tried to go slower, but that didn't stop the popping so much as make it sound more ominous. She decided to slide forward on her stomach instead. It wasn't quite as convenient as crawling, but it made a lot less noise.

When Monica reached the last shaft, the one that should stretch out directly over Newt's secret lab, she paused. Again she worried that this was all a bit *too easy.*

She climbed into the shaft and found the vent facing down into the lab. Through the slats, she could see Newt's lair.

The floor of the place was covered with sparkling white tiles—the kind you'd find in a hospital room. Against the walls were dozens of electronic machines covered in dials and knobs. On a rolling cart below were an open can of soda and a half-eaten candied apple—part of Newt's dinner, no doubt. On another, there was some kind of remote control device. One Monica had never seen before.

She unscrewed the vent cover and slid it out of the way. She stuck her head down in the opening, expecting to spy Newt in one of the corners, hard at work on his robot.

Monica gasped. Newt was in the room, all right— looking directly at her.

"Hello, Monica," he said.

As if on cue, the section of the shaft she was in dropped out from under her. She fell into a large safety net. Newt pulled a drawstring and the entire net snapped shut, trapping her inside.

"Newt Lizzard," Monica said, as soon as she caught her breath, "I appreciate you catching me, but you better have a really good explanation for why you knew I'd be falling!"

"Monica, Monica, Monica." Newt had an awful grin on his chubby face. "Do you really have time for the whole *megillah*?"

"If you don't cut it out with the Yiddish," she threatened, "I'm going to sock you in the nose!"

Monica lashed around in the net, as if she might break

free and give Newt the thumping she'd threatened. Unfortunately, she only got herself more entangled.

"I'm just trying to speak your language, *bubbeleh*," Newt continued. "And I don't imagine it will be easy for you to sock anyone in the nose, considering your current situation."

He picked up the remote control and pressed a button. Monica's net rose into the air. It was connected to a crane and some kind of pulley system that led across the room— all the way over to what looked like an operating table.

"What's going on here?" Monica demanded.

"Well, I was going to tell you. But then you started threatening me, so I've changed my mind. Until the main event, I'll just let you *hang out* for a while. Ha ha. *Hang out*. That's funny, isn't it?"

"Hilarious." Monica sighed. "Newt, I'm sorry for threatening you. Now tell me what you're up to or *you'll* be sorry."

Newt put down the remote and checked the gauges on the machines against the wall. "Fine. I'll indulge you. Where should I start? I suppose you know by now that I'm behind the blackout. And you are aware of my plans to transform TOAD into a real human being. I'm absolutely positive Kev1n and BB told you about it, or you never would have come out here looking for me. As for the net and the table, well, maybe you think I'm some kind of Dr. Frankenstein?"

"I think you're a *shmendrik*." Monica spat the words.

Newt picked up the remote and hit one of the buttons, and the crane started moving toward the gurney again.

"Okay, okay," Monica pleaded. "Wait. You're not a *shmendrik*. But none of what BB and Kev1n told me explains why you've trapped me in this stupid net."

"Are you sure you want to know?" He gazed up at her, not saying anything for a few moments. There was a look in his eyes that vaguely resembled sympathy.

Being on the receiving end of Newt Lizzard's sympathy made Monica slightly ill.

"The thing is," Newt finally continued, "creating an android that's even remotely similar to a real kid is not so simple. But if you study hard and have some brains, it's also not impossible. It's just . . . there's a *catch*. All those muscles that make Kev1n so agile or you capable of playing the violin so well, they're not easy to copy mechanically. The same with all the organs that allow us to digest food and fuel those muscles. Our skin, tongues, ears, eyes—all of those things are highly complex."

"What are you getting at?" Monica asked.

"What I'm getting at is that it's nearly impossible to create a human body out of bolts and screws, microchips and copper wires. But taking a preexisting human body and adding to it, that's another story!"

"Preexisting . . . ? You mean *me*?" Monica shrieked.

"Yes. Your brain. Your body. Your DNA. Congratulations, Monica. You've been chosen to participate in the most exciting scientific experiment of all time. A quick grafting of Dr. Park's organic metal, a download of TOAD's programming into your brain—and *shazzam!* TOAD is real. I'll never be lonely again."

"So you make a robot. But what about *me*?" Monica asked. "What happens to *me*?"

"Like I said, you will be converted . . ."

"No, I mean *me*. The me who plays violin and hates outdoor sports and is friends with BB and Kev1n," Monica clarified.

"Oh," Newt said, looking down at his feet. "You really don't want to know."

"Meaning?"

"Meaning there won't be any *you* tomorrow to be mad at *me*." With that, Newt returned to his equipment, checking connections and plugging things in.

Monica digested Newt's words, then decided she'd had enough. She was not going to be part of any of Newt's cockamamie experiments.

She reached behind her back and began running her fingers along the net. She had such a well-developed sense of touch from all those years playing her Stradivarius that she could feel the weakness in a string days before it broke. Somewhere there would be a spot in the net that hadn't been tied well or that was just a little too loose.

Aha! Monica found what she wanted. She pulled on the nearby strings in one direction, then the other. She could feel the net beginning to unravel.

It was just a matter of time.

Monica only hoped she had enough of it left.

16

TRAFFIC JAMS

TOAD," BB asked as he pedaled, "what's the quickest route to Newt's secret lab?"

TOAD's voice sounded through the vid-pod. "I suggest you bicycle through the center of Manhattan, taking Fifth Avenue all the way to Central Park and then east on Fifty-ninth Street to the Queensboro Bridge."

"That's a horrible idea," Kev1n said. "The traffic on Fifth Avenue will be bumper-to-bumper."

"The traffic on Fifth Avenue may be bad," TOAD explained. "I do not have that information because of the electrical outage. But I predict there will be a high police presence in that area of town, which, among other things, will expedite your trip."

"Sure," BB said, "lots of uniforms because of all the fancy shops. But how will that make our trip go by more quickly?"

"Because," TOAD continued, "the traffic and crowds will be much more orderly. Altogether, I predict you will make better time by taking that route."

Kev1n narrowed his eyes. BB knew that he still didn't trust TOAD completely. As much as the computer had helped them, it seemed unlikely that he had given up on his hopes of being placed in an actual human body.

"No way," Kev1n told BB. "Let's take First Avenue. That'll take us right to the bridge and then we'll be almost there."

They took the route Kev1n suggested and had hardly pedaled five blocks along First Avenue when the crowd grew thick. So thick they could barely move. It was like playing bumper cars, only the cars were people who didn't really enjoy it when a kid on a bicycle rammed into them.

When they finally made it to the Queensboro Bridge, it seemed impossible that they would arrive at the warehouse in time to help Monica.

"TOAD," BB said into his vid-pod. "Are you there?"

"I am here. Not that I am capable of gloating, but it appears you made a very bad navigational decision. I am afraid your time is quickly running out."

"Yes, we know," BB continued. "And we're really sorry we didn't trust you. Right, Kev1n?"

"Terribly sorry," Kev1n answered.

"That is fine," TOAD answered. "I am not the kind of computer to hold a grudge."

"Thank you," BB said. "But isn't there something else you can do? I mean, can't you stop Newt or slow him down or at least tell us what's going on right now?"

"Currently Newt Lizzard and Monica Steen are involved in hand-to-hand combat. I can see this on the security cameras in the laboratory."

"What?" Kev1n laughed. "Newt's no match for Monica. He's no match for anybody."

"You should not underestimate Newt Lizzard's strength," TOAD argued. "While he has a history of overeating, he comes from very athletic parents. Besides, he is devoted to his plans and this gives him an advantage. My prediction is that he will win the fight."

"Then you've got to do something to help her," BB demanded.

"I have already done more than I should."

"Please, TOAD," Kev1n begged.

"One moment . . ."

Kev1n and BB continued bicycling across the bridge. Kev1n wove in and out of the cars, hopping up onto curbs and off. BB, on the other hand, kept his eyes ahead, pedaling as fast as he could. He didn't want to run into the back of a car. Doing so would send him flying off his bicycle head over heels. And a broken collarbone would *not* help them save Monica.

Finally TOAD came back over the vid-pod. "I have done all I can," he said. "The rest will be up to the two of you—and Monica herself."

"What exactly have you done?" Kev1n asked.

"There is a key program," TOAD explained, "which Newt has named Mind Meld. It is the program that would transfer my system, my memory, into whatever subject ends up on Newt's table. I have disabled it . . . but that is all it is within my power to do. The mechanical aspect of the program—the part that fuses the organic metal to the human subject—is still online. It is controlled by a physical switch located inside the laboratory. It would require someone with an actual body to disable it. As you well know, a physical body is something I do not have."

"So Monica's in the clear?" BB asked.

"No. If Monica loses her fight with Newt and he places her under the transformer console, she will still need to survive the process of having the organic metal grafted to her skin."

"Meaning she'll end up with what? Like a permanent armor? An aluminum foil bodysuit?" Kev1n asked. "That doesn't sound so bad. Actually, it sounds pretty cool."

"No," TOAD told the boys. "The process would be very dangerous. The process was never intended to salvage the human subject. She may end up, as they say, a vegetable—though a heavily armored vegetable. I do not know if this will be 'cool' or not."

BB turned to Kev1n. "Hurry! We don't have much time!"

Kev1n jetted down the bridge's roadway. BB took a deep breath and pedaled—faster than he ever had before.

17

THE BATTLE

When Monica escaped from the net, she did just what she had threatened—socked Newt Lizzard in the nose.

For a moment, it seemed entirely possible that the whole ordeal had come to an end. Newt fell to the floor hard, put his hands over his face, and began shaking.

"Hey. I didn't want to hit you," Monica said, moving a little closer. "I hope you're all right."

She stood over him, trying to see if he was bleeding. "Oh, come on, Newt. Don't cry. It's just that, well, you were going to turn me into some kind of android. I didn't have any choice."

She reached down to pull his hands away from his face

and gasped when she realized he wasn't crying, but grinning.

Newt kicked his leg and swept Monica's feet out from under her. She fell and Newt immediately jumped up. "It's not going to be *that* easy," he told her.

Monica climbed to her feet and again swung for the boy's nose. But this time, he was ready. He ducked. As her fist whizzed above his head, Newt grabbed her shoelaces and yanked on them. Monica lost her balance and fell backward—landing right on top of Newt's operating table.

To her left and right, she could see big leather belts—the kind hospitals used to strap down mental patients. She took a deep breath, gathering her strength to continue the battle.

She sat up and found Newt pointing his remote control in her face.

"Don't move," Newt warned. "This is a laser blaster. I can vaporize you in two seconds."

"No fair," Monica whined.

"Fair?" Newt answered, a sneer on his face. "This isn't a *game*, Monica. Far from it. Now be nice and I won't have to use those straps."

"Why should I cooperate with you?" Monica asked. "It's not like you can shoot me."

Newt raised an eyebrow. "No? Why not?"

"Because a dead body won't work for your experiment. If it did, you could have stolen one from the morgue. You need someone *alive*. Right, Dr. Frankenstein?"

Monica jumped off the table and lunged at Newt.

He fired the laser blaster, and Monica felt a flash of heat.

"Hey!" she said, catching a whiff of a horrible burning odor. "My hair! You singed my hair!"

"Listen, Monica," Newt said, moving so that now the table was between them, "I think it's time we had a little talk."

"Newt, I'm sorry, but I am so *not* going to be your girlfriend," Monica deadpanned.

"Very funny, but the time for jokes is over. I'd rather not shoot you, but you are mistaken to think it would be impossible for me to do so. Listen. I know you have excellent hearing. What do you hear?"

She looked up at the ceiling and tried to make out the sound. It sounded like something—or some *things*—scurrying around in the ventilation ducts.

"I don't know, Newt. Rats?" she guessed. "Is your father's warehouse infested with rats? That doesn't scare me. I'm a city girl, remember?"

Newt slowly shook his head. "Not rats. Listen again."

Monica focused on the sound coming from above them.

Definitely something moving around, she thought, *but something a lot heavier than rats . . .*

In an instant, she had it. "BB and Kev1n!" she cheered. "They're here to kick your butt and rescue me!"

"Mazel tov, Monica," Newt said. "Good job, but not quite."

He again aimed the weapon at her head. "Are you ready to listen to me now?"

"Go ahead."

"That sound of someone crawling through the ventilation shafts *is* BB and Kev1n. But they're not your rescue squad. They're my backup plan. I figured they would eventually escape from the closet in the lab. The three of you are very crafty that way. So if you do give me a hard time, *I will shoot you*. Then I will reset my net, trap BB and Kev1n, and use one of *them* for my experiment. How does that sound?"

"You wouldn't."

"Try me. Although it will be an awful waste to not only sacrifice yourself but your two friends in the process."

Monica had no idea if Newt would really shoot her or not. And she didn't want to find out. She also didn't want to put BB and Kev1n at any more risk. At least if she played along, she'd buy everybody a little time.

"Fine. I'll cooperate," she said, "if you promise not to hurt BB or Kev1n."

"I promise."

"Okay. What do I do?"

"Get back on the table."

Monica climbed up on the table and lay down. Very slowly, Newt approached her and started fastening the straps.

"Hey," she said, "I thought you weren't going to tie me down."

"That was before. I'm not sure I can trust you now."

"*You're* not sure you can trust *me*? *Feh*. If that isn't the pot calling the kettle black."

Newt strapped her to the table and rolled it into the spot directly below the transformer, a huge device that looked like an overgrown lightbulb. Monica knew her situation was dire. She had to distract him.

"Newt, please don't do this."

"Honestly," he said, "you should try to relax. It'll be less painful that way. Just imagine you're at the dentist."

"Oh, sure. Because that's relaxing."

Newt walked over to a computer and typed in a few commands, then rechecked his gauges and dials. He walked over to the wall and put his hand on a large switch.

"Wait!" Monica screamed.

"What?"

"There's somebody outside the door. Can't you hear them?"

"No, there's not. BB and Kev1n are still lost in the ventilation ducts. I can track them by the vid-pods they're wearing."

"Still. Somebody's there. I can hear them."

"No," he said. "You're wrong." He began to count down. "Ten, nine, eight—"

"Newt!" Monica screamed.

"Seven, six . . ."

"Wait!"

He grasped the lever tighter, then paused, deep in thought.

To Monica, it seemed like he was experiencing a final pang of guilt over what he was going do to.

Then he frowned.

Monica squeezed her eyes shut as Newt Lizzard prepared to throw the switch.

18

LOST IN A LABYRINTH

When BB and Kev1n arrived at the warehouse, Kev1n pointed out Monica's bicycle, leaning against the fence.

"And look," he told BB. "See that drum and crate piled up? I bet that's where she climbed into the ventilation duct."

They crossed the empty lot and climbed up and into the duct.

"Okay," Kev1n said once they were inside. "Which way?"

BB touched the buttons on his vid-pod. He stared at the screen, totally confused.

"What's wrong?" Kev1n asked.

"The plans . . . they're gone!"

"Can't you download them again?" Kev1n asked.

"I'm trying, but there's all sorts of new security around the web site. I can't get in."

"Great. So now what do we do?" Kev1n asked.

"I guess we find the way to the lab on our own," BB suggested.

The two of them crawled through the ventilation shafts. At first, they could follow Monica's path through the dust on the shaft's floor. But before long, they were totally lost.

"Hey," Kev1n said, "maybe we'd have better luck finding Newt's lab from the ground, going room to room. At least then we'd be able to tell where we've been. Unlike here, where all the shafts look identical."

Kev1n unscrewed the vent cover before them and slipped down into the room below. When he looked up, he could see BB peeking over the edge of the opening.

"You know, Kev," BB said. "That's, like, a really long jump. I mean, it looks kinda high from up here and I'm, well, a little . . ."

"You're what? Dude, you're not scared, are you?" Kev1n scoffed.

"I don't like heights, okay?" BB admitted.

"Heights? It's not even ten feet."

"Well, not all of us were born with your crazy athletic ability," BB argued.

"Come on. Falling is easy. Gravity totally does the work."

"Funny," BB snarled, "but not helpful."

"Okay, I have an idea," Kev1n told him. "Why don't you hang down, you know, holding on to the ledge. You're almost five feet tall, right? So when you let go, you'll only have another four or five feet to drop. It'll be cake."

BB, having no other choice, took Kev1n's advice. He slid his feet and legs out over the ledge, then shimmied the rest of his body until he was hanging down, holding on only by the tips of his fingers. . . .

"Okay." BB closed his eyes. "Here goes."

At that moment, a scream echoed through the shaft.

"Monica!" Kev1n said.

"Back in the vent!" BB called. "Back in the vent! Push me up!"

Kev1n pushed him up by the soles of his feet, then grabbed BB's hand and swung himself into the duct.

They heard another scream. The sound came from an

opening in the shaft just a few feet away. They could see light beaming up through the opening.

Kev1n and BB crawled toward the sound as fast as they could.

When they got to the opening and looked down into it, they saw lots of machinery and equipment, the smelting device from Dr. Park's laboratory, and tables and chairs that had clearly been knocked over during a struggle.

Newt's lab. There was no doubt about it.

"Where's Monica?" BB asked.

"I don't know, but look."

Newt stood below them, beside a huge switch on the wall.

"He's going to meld her!" Kev1n said.

BB took in the scene. He spied a rolling cart, with a candied apple sitting on top of it, directly below the vent.

"Don't worry, Kev. I have a plan," he said. "Just follow me."

19

ANKLE BRACELET

Ankara arrived outside the warehouse and saw three bicycles leaning against the fence. She also saw a place where the security gate had been pulled back.

"I don't think I'm going to fit through that opening," she told her driver.

"I could try to pull it farther back," Sener offered. He tugged on the opening, trying his best to make it larger.

"Not enough leverage. Maybe something else." He went to his bicycle taxi and pulled a length of rope out from under the seat.

"You don't expect me to climb *over* the razor wire, do you?" Ankara asked.

Sener shook his head and smiled. "Not at all, my Turkish flower." He tied one end of the rope to the fence where it had been pulled back and the other to the back of his taxi. Then he climbed on the bicycle, backed up a few feet, and pedaled forward as fast as he could.

The rope went taut—and the taxi screeched to a halt, nearly shooting Sener out of his seat.

Ankara gazed at the opening. It was no larger than it had been before.

"I think we need a bit more weight," Sener said. He looked at Ankara, then glanced quickly away.

"More weight?" she asked.

"Yes, if you would just sit in the carriage once more . . ."

Ankara gasped. "You're not suggesting that I'm . . . I'm *fat*, are you?"

"No, nothing of the sort," Sener broke in. "A *little* more weight. That should be more than enough."

"Herhangí," Ankara said. Which in Turkish basically meant, *Whatever.*

Ankara sat in the carriage and again Sener backed up his taxi.

He pedaled forward. The rope went taut—

And this time, the fence ripped away from its

frame. The hole left was large enough to drive a car through.

"Wonderful," Ankara cheered. "Now if you don't mind waiting here for a few moments, I need to retrieve a certain young man."

20

THE SWITCH

Newt could feel the lever's cold metal under his hand. He could hear Monica yelling at him, but her words no longer made sense. He could even hear himself counting down from ten, but somehow it seemed like the voice was coming from outside himself. He couldn't believe it. In seconds, all his dreams would come true.

He gripped the switch tighter. He felt the muscles in his arm tense. Yet . . .

Something was wrong. He couldn't pull the switch.

He heard himself say, "Two, one, zero . . ." And at zero, he just stood there, holding the switch, *not* pulling it.

Why couldn't he pull it? He wasn't sure, but in those

fleeting moments unexpected thoughts passed through his head—thoughts of all the people who would be hurt if there were explosions, thoughts of the terrible injury he'd be doing to Monica.

Newt hung his head. In a whisper that no one could hear but himself, he said, "I can't. I can't do it."

And then he heard a familiar voice behind him.

"Newt Lizzard," his nanny said, "what do you think you're doing?"

"Ankle Bracelet? I . . . um . . . what are *you* doing here?"

"I'm here," the woman said, "because that's what I do—keep up with you and try my best to stop you from getting into trouble. But it's not me who should be doing the explaining. What are *you* doing here?"

"I don't know, Ankle Bracelet. I mean, it's that TOAD . . . You know. . . ."

"Yes, yes. I read all about your plans to make a robot. Sounds to me like you've been watching too much television."

"But Ankle . . ."

"Don't 'Ankle' me," she told the boy, giving him a stern look. "And why do you have that poor girl tied up? You have better manners than that."

Ankara went over to the table onto which Newt had strapped Monica. "It's okay, sweetie," she said to Monica as she began undoing the straps. Then she looked back at Newt. "Now, Newt Lizzard, I want you to come away from that switch right now. I've heard just about all I want to hear about robots."

Newt's bottom lip started shaking and his eyes watered up. He felt like he was going to cry. Something had gone very wrong. And it wasn't just that his plans had been ruined. It was also that he had discovered something new about himself. He felt a terrible hurt welling up inside.

"But Ankle Bracelet," he said, "I . . . I just wanted someone to love me!"

"But Newt, honey," Ankara told him. *I love you.*

Monica rubbed her wrists and hopped up from the table. "Don't cry, Newt. I heard what you said. I know that you couldn't go through with it."

Ankara blinked. "He couldn't?"

"No," Monica confirmed. "At the very last minute, Newt changed his mind!"

Ankara beamed. "Oh, sweetie. I'm so proud of you! You *are* a good boy."

Newt turned his back in shame.

"You probably hate me now," he mumbled to Monica.

"Well, you were kind of a *schlemiel*," she began.

"I know. And I'd do anything to take it back," Newt told her, his voice quivering.

"Well, why don't we—"

Out of the corner of her eye, Monica noticed two heads popping out of the ventilation shaft.

"Kev1n! BB!" she called.

The two boys dropped down to the floor.

"Don't worry, Monica!" Kev1n called.

"We're here to save you!" BB chimed in.

They grabbed the rolling cart that was standing beside them. With a yell, they ran toward Newt as fast as they could.

They stopped short—and the cart shrieked across the vinyl floor—toward Newt's pudgy little figure.

Ankara Braceling gasped.

"No!" Monica cried.

Wham! The cart hit Newt square in the back. He began to fall.

And Monica realized that he was *still* grasping the switch!

"Look out!" she cried.

She dove to the floor just as the dial clicked into the on position.

There was a blinding flash of light, then all the lights in the room went dark.

21

SYSTEM OVERLOAD

A million trillion watts of power flowed through the system. The metal-cell grafting process had been initiated—on Ankara Braceling.

A few moments later, the fail-safes tripped. The system shut down and the grafting process terminated. A second after that, all the lights in the room blinked on.

Everyone stared at Ankara. She looked dazed, her face was a little gray, and her hair stood on end.

Newt's heart felt like it had stopped.

"Ankle!" he yelped. "Are you all right?"

Ankara blinked. Coughed. "All right?" she repeated. "I'm fine. Actually, I've never felt better!"

Newt eyed her warily. "Any effects from the blast?"

Ankara whirled her arms around and bent her legs—once, twice, three times. "Hmm," she said. "I do feel a little tingly in the shoulders. But I'm certainly not *hurt*."

Newt let out a tremendous sigh as Monica whirled on her two best friends. "Just what did you think you were doing?"

"We were, uh, saving you from Newt?" Kev1n ventured.

"Saving me? *Saving me?*" Monica asked. "You could have killed me and Ankara!"

"But he was going to turn you into a robot," BB insisted.

Monica threw her hands in the air. "No, he wasn't!"

From his place across the room, Newt cleared his throat. "Well, actually, I was. I just couldn't go through with it."

"See, geniuses?" Monica continued. "Newt's not a bad guy after all."

"Aha!" BB shouted. He leapt in the air, pointed in Kev1n's face. "I knew it! I knew it! I was right all along!"

Newt stared up at his transformation machine.

Ankle was okay, which meant something in his program hadn't gone according to plan. He peered at the computer screen above him and saw TOAD's face.

Suddenly it all made sense.

"You turned it off?" Newt asked his computer. "You turned off the program that would make you real. Why?"

"You know the answer to that," the computer responded. "You programmed me. I could never intentionally harm a human being. My code would not allow it—no more than your code would."

"But we had such great plans," Newt cried. "We were going to have ice cream together. And take over the world!"

"No, you couldn't pull the switch in the end—"

"You're right." Newt pouted.

The face on the computer screen now smiled widely. "You see, we're even more similar than you imagined. You, Newt, are me. And I am you. So in a way, I am already real. All the qualities you programmed into me to make the best friend ever—they already exist in you."

"That's right," Ankara said to Newt, "you're already a great boy."

She went over to him and put her arms around him. She gave him a squeeze.

"Ouch. Hey," Newt said, trying to pull away from her.

"What, you're not too big for a hug from your old nanny, are you?"

"No," he answered, gasping for breath. "But that's a *really* powerful hug."

Ankara smiled and let him go.

Kev1n, BB, and Monica grinned at each other.

"Seriously, Mon. You okay?" BB asked.

"I'm fine," Monica answered.

Kev1n gave her a light punch on the shoulder. "Welcome back."

He turned to Newt. "And, uh, sorry about the cart thing."

"No harm done," Newt said, a rueful smile on his face. "Sorry about the closet."

Kev1n held up a hand and shook his head. "Bygones."

"Well," BB started. "I think it's time the Blackout Gang got back to Pine Rock Mountain. Boring or not, it's the perfect place to get a little much-needed rest!"

"Uh, yeah," Newt told him, his face turning red. "Except—the electricity is still out. There are no trains. Remember?"

"Pine Rock Mountain?" Ankara said. "Are the three of you playing hooky from summer camp?"

"Well." Kev1n shrugged. "Sorta."

"Then I suggest you spent the night at your homes. In fact, I'll be calling all your parents to make sure you do exactly that."

"Um, Ankle Bracelet?" Newt broke in. "I sent their parents away on vacation."

"You did, did you? Then perhaps you should invite your new friends to spend the night at *your* house."

Newt glanced at the three of them and tried to smile. "Well," he said, as meekly as he'd ever spoken in his entire life. "Wanna?"

BB, Kev1n, and Monica looked at each other and shrugged. Did they really want to spend the night at Lizzard Mansion? After everything that had happened?

"Okay," Kev1n said. "But *only* if I get to check out the skate park on the roof."

"And only if we don't have to sleep in the reptile room," Monica added.

"And maybe you can show me how you hacked into all those company mainframes?" BB asked.

"No computers!" Ankara answered them. "I can, however, assure you that Newt Lizzard will be the absolute best host ever. And if you're all nice children, I'll see that everyone gets dessert before bed. Lots and lots of dessert."

They agreed and turned to leave, with Ankara leading the way.

But when she opened the door to the lab, the steel knob shrieked—and twisted free in her grip!

The Blackout Gang looked at Newt and then at Ankara. A grin formed on the old woman's lined face.

"Um, Newt? Does Ankara's skin look—kind of *sparkly* to you?" Monica asked.

Newt gulped, nodded. "The metal-melding process. It seems to have—"

"Whoa!" BB interrupted. "Newt's nanny has super-human strength."

Newt smiled. "My experiment. It worked. Sort of."

"Well, now," Ankara said. "That could certainly come in handy."

EPILOGUE

O ver the next few weeks, rumors circulated about just what—or who—was behind the mysterious power failure.

Some blamed it on terrorists. Some accused the electric companies. And some mentioned a shadowy group of twelve-year-olds who hadn't prevented the blackout but who stopped it from getting *much* worse.

"Listen to this," Kev1n said.

The three of them sat in his living room in Manhattan as he read from his computer screen.

"'The unconfirmed rumor is that an unknown person stole the electricity for his own nefarious purposes. Our sources say that he was stopped by three children calling themselves the Manhattan Musketeers.'"

"The *what*?" Monica asked. "That's an awful name!"

"Where are you reading that?" BB asked.

"Where else?" Kev1n smirked. "The *Post*'s web site."

"Great. Pass me my laptop."

Kev1n did just that. For about thirty seconds, BB typed away at the keyboard. Then he looked up at Kev1n. "Read it again."

Kev1n scrolled down his own screen and reread the end of the article. "'Our sources say that he was stopped by three twelve-year-old geniuses, now almost universally known as the Blackout Gang.'"

Kev1n smiled. "Awesome."

BB shrugged. "What good are a bunch of super-kids without a super-cool name?"

Monica lifted her soda. "To the Blackout Gang!"

Kev1n and BB lifted their own. "To the Blackout Gang!" they answered.